D0866327

LIFE IS A STRANGE PLACE
A novel by Frank Turner Hollon

MacAdam/Cage
155 Sansome Street, Suite 550
San Francisco, CA 94104
www.macadamcage.com

Library of Congress Cataloging-in-Publication Data

Hollon, Frank Turner, 1963—
Life is a strange place : a novel / by Frank Turner Hollon.
p. cm.
ISBN 1-931561-47-8 (hardcover : alk. paper)
1. Life change events—Fiction. 2. Loss (Psychology)—Fiction.
3. Misogyny—Fiction 4. Testis—Fiction 5. Men—Fiction. I. Title.

PS3608.O494L54 2003
813'.6—dc21

                                          2003013009

Manufactured in the United States of America
10 9 8 7 6 5 4 3 2 1

Book design by Dorothy Carico Smith.

LIFE IS A STRANGE PLACE
A novel by Frank Turner Hollon

MacAdam/Cage

For my wife, Allison, and Dusty and Mary Grace

He that lives upon Hope,
dies Farting.

–Benjamin Franklin
FOUNDING FATHER
OF THE UNITED STATES OF AMERICA

Poor Richard's Almanack, 1736

CHAPTER ONE

THE DEVOTION TO LEG

I can't imagine living for anything other than women. The devotion to leg is an instinct I am not inclined to suppress nor even control other than to try to keep the wheels between the lines of the law and common decency. What is it about that crevice deserving of such reverence and utter minute-by-minute attention? I don't know, and I don't care.

A moment exists in the spire of the universe at the edge of sexual success for which there is no equal. Food is no substitute, or sports, or a career. It is the moment exactly after uncertainty and immediately preceding touching the gold. I ponder the exhilaration of that moment as I write these words that cannot possibly describe the feeling. I can only hope to create parameters for your own memory and imagination.

It is with this in mind that I relate the events leading up to the involuntary removal of my testicles.

She was about sixteen. Too young to desire, but I could not pretend I didn't. At thirty-three years old, I was the same age as Jesus when he died, and I was losing a little hair and my options for attracting women had narrowed a bit. The knowledge of this narrowing only seemed to goose me toward the girls who now called me "Sir," who whispered to each other when I gave the Stare. Never underestimate the Stare. It can win the moment or it can cause a cosmic disturbance that leaves me feeling like a red-nosed clown with big fat red shoes.

When I saw Candice that day in the mall I had no time to calculate the Stare. It came out on its own, pure, honest, and fueled by the devotion to leg. She smiled back an instant too long. Just an instant. You have to understand the signs. Unless you've dedicated yourself to this little piece of the world, you won't understand. For instance, when a married woman is attracted to a man she sees, she will touch her wedding ring with her other hand. It isn't a conscious reaction. Instead, it's a subconscious attempt to reassure herself and play strong. Or maybe it's a signal for this new tiger to take a step back. But it's something. And you've got to see it, interpret its meaning, right or wrong, and act upon her instruction. I digress.

Candice smiled too long. I said, "Hello."

She said, "Hello."

Doesn't sound like much, but I knew several things immediately. First, she liked me. Second, she wanted me to know it. Third, she was bored with this day and felt a primal urge to push the edge of her teenage envelope. Her blue jeans were tight, and I stepped back to let her in the line ahead of me. Not only was it the gentlemanly thing to do, but I would be able to listen to her tell the man behind the glass booth which movie she would be seeing. It was a matinee. I love matinees. I had already seen the movie she selected, but I bought a ticket anyway and we moved to the popcorn line. We both stared up at the price list.

I said, "It's ridiculous how much a Coke costs at the movies."

She giggled. I wanted to dance a jig. The jig of hope.

"My name's Barry."

"Hi, Barry. I'm Candice." Her little nose was perfect on her perfect skin above her shiny little lips. Her eyes were big and brown and she looked away back to the price list.

I bought her a Coke. Suddenly I felt like a little boy, hanging on her next expression, dangling images of porcelain nakedness twirling around in my open mind. We sat down in the semidarkness, too close to the screen for my eyes. The few other people in the theater sat near the back.

"This movie got a good review in the Sunday paper," I said.

"Who reads the Sunday paper?" she said.

Not me.

"Do you have a boyfriend?"

She smiled, "You remind me of my Uncle Randy."

What kind of crazy shit is that to say, I thought.

We sat silent for a few minutes.

Candice said, "Barry, if I told you right now that you will never, ever, get your hands in my pants, here, now, anywhere, never, would you still talk to me?"

As she finished the question the lights lowered and the big screen jumped to life. I've been doing this too long to laugh at a question like that. Just the fact that the question exists inches me closer to that moment of exhilaration and ultimate golden pleasure.

"Talk about what?" I asked.

She laughed, soft and funny, and then reached her hand in the dark to my lap. The reaction was instant. Bodily fluids focused, rushed, and congregated like armies of color. Her hand flexed slightly, almost not at all, and then squeezed.

Of course, as I write this now, I know it sounds too

good to be true. At the time it didn't seem so unbelievable. When you spend your days and nights digging in the desert for gold, how surprised should you be the day you find it? I mean, on occasion I've worked a barroom asking politely each woman to go home with me. My experience reveals that one out of ten will just say "Yes." More want to, but they let other factors interfere. What will people think of me? Maybe he's a killer.

When she pulled down my zipper my head instinctively turned left and then right to make sure the coast was clear. Before I could count my blessings her pretty little hand with the painted nails had my best friend out dancing in the soft light of the idiotic previews on the screen. As I was beginning to fully appreciate the moment, a flashlight came out of the dark and lit up my private parts like a bulldog in the headlights.

"What the hell's going on here?" the man's voice boomed.

I heard myself say, "Oh, shit!" I knew somehow I would remember this single slice of time in my life with the size and clarity of the movie on the screen in front of me.

It was Candice's father. At least I think her name was Candice. The man stood in the flickering light, a flashlight in one hand, and oddly, a brass trumpet in the other hand. I remember thinking, "Why would a person bring a trumpet to the theater?" I turned to Candice. There was no expression on her face. None. She simply turned her head to the movie, and before I could move I felt an implosion of pain from my testicles like Great Satan's red-hot pitchfork thrusting up my rectum. The man had blasted me with all of his might in the crotch with the small end of the brass trumpet against the vulnerability of my pitiful nuts. My vision left me instantly. I rolled forward and onto the sticky floor with bits of popcorn and Jujubes. The insides of my body pulled together like tight rubber bands wrapped around the core. I couldn't hear, but somehow felt a cool strip of saliva easing slowly from the corner of my open mouth and down to the place where my cheek rested against the dirty black floor.

When I came to my senses I was in a hospital. There was a dull pain down below and a nurse by the bed. My mother was in the room.

"Barry? Barry, you're awake."

The memory of the theater existed like a dream I couldn't quite pull back together.

I heard my mother say, "You've had an operation. The doctor says everything will be O.K."

I repeated, "Operation?"

"Honey, what happened? They said they found you on the floor at the matinee. What on Earth happened?"

Candice's face flashed clear and sweet. The memories slowly drifted back together and focused. The doctor came in the room.

"Barry."

"Yes."

"We had to remove both testicles, Barry. I thought we could save the left one, but it was simply too ruptured. Can you tell me what happened?"

I thought about explaining everything, maybe leaving out a few details, but it can't be explained. What's the use? I lost my balls. The father of a sixteen-year-old girl caught me in a theater with his daughter's hand on my penis and he gouged me in the nuts with a musical instrument so hard that they had to take them off and throw them away. My story begins.

CHAPTER TWO

LIDA GRIGGS

I know what you're saying. How could a man get hit in the balls with such force that they must be permanently removed? I don't know the answer. All I know is my testicles are gone. I can't get them back. Right now they're probably lying side by side in some medical waste junkyard wondering where the rest of me has gone.

My girlfriend, Lida Griggs, was out of town when the incident occurred. I call her my girlfriend, but the term is a stretch of reality. We don't see each other for weeks or months at a time. She'll just show up one day, walk in my door, and act like we've never been apart. I'm not sure we even like each other.

Lida has a dog named "Boner" she believes to be her soul mate. She has no concept of the name and seems not to notice when people giggle or glance sideways at one another when introduced to this monstrous Great Dane with a head bigger than mine. She has some stupid story about how he buried a porkchop bone in the backyard when he was just a puppy. Hence, the name "Boner."

I hate him. She calls me "Daddy" around him and insists I kiss the beefy dog on the top of his oversized head every time we're reintroduced. I've seen her kiss him on the lips just minutes after he sat in the corner licking his dog parts like they were candy.

"How can you do that?" I asked once.

"Don't be silly," she said.

How do you talk sense to somebody who thinks it's

not gross to kiss a dog on his mouth after he licks himself? You can't. You can't talk sense to them, you can't break up with them, and for God's sake you can't turn them away when they've got an ass like Lida's. Smooth and curvaceous, a perfect package in tight shorts.

I stayed in the hospital for several days before I went home. For a week my crazy mother came over every day to cook my meals and make sure I took my medicine. She continued to bring me dinner for months. When I finally went back to work I made up a story about a botched hernia operation which included an infection and possible legal action. They bought it.

And then Lida knocked on the door. She tried the doorknob first and only knocked because it was locked. I thought about sitting on the couch until she went away, but Lida's not the kind of woman who goes away gently. For weeks I'd been rehearsing how to explain my missing parts. I even considered the possibility of prosthetic testicles and no explanation at all.

In she came, Boner in tow, with that big fat purse over her shoulder.

The first thing out of her mouth was, "So where have you been, Mister?"

Her voice was sharp and accusatory, laced with evil undertones. I was too tired and depressed to even take the time to care. My medicine made me slow.

"Say hello to your son," she said.

"Hello, Boner."

I think the dog hated me as much as I hated him. He probably had dog dreams of chasing me down and ripping the soft flesh from my neck.

The next thing I knew Lida had changed her tone and took me by the hand to lead me to the bedroom. This wasn't unusual, but under the present circumstances, my mind raced. For the first time in my entire life the exhilaration of imminent sex was buried in a huge pile of anxiety and other mental feces.

We kissed once and then twice, open-mouthed, which suddenly seemed disgusting. Lida sat me down on the edge of the bed and excused herself to the bathroom. The giant dog stood guard at the bedroom door like a royal wolfhound. I took a deep breath as we stared at each other and hoped some horrific catastrophe would occur. My mind was numb, and my body was heavy and tired.

I heard myself say to the dog, "Please God, do something."

Lida came out of the bathroom wearing a baby doll powder blue love garment. On a normal day I would have come out of my shoes to unwrap her present, but it wasn't a normal day.

The angry look was back in her eye. She turned off the lights and pushed me back onto the bed. My pants were the first to go, and then my shirt. She was rough and pushy, practically dragging me to the center of the bed.

She bit the edge of my ear and whispered, "Today we're gonna do something new, lover."

"Lida, I really don't feel very well. I think I might have a virus."

She ignored me and reached down by the side of the bed to her giant purse. She moved fast forward, and I felt a nylon rope around my wrist. She was tying and knotting my hands to the headboard. There was no energy to fight.

I just wanted it over. Soon she would find out the awful truth, and then maybe she would go away and take that stupid dog out of my room.

She was strong like a man, and I imagined for a moment that she was a man, and somehow I hadn't noticed before, and she was tying me up to take pictures of me for some homosexual Internet porno site.

And then she was finished. My wrists were tied tight to opposite ends of the headboard and my ankles were tied to the bedposts, spread-eagle and naked like the day I was born, except, of course, for my missing gonads.

When the light came on the dog had moved next to the side of the bed with his face a few feet from my face. Lida was digging through the bottomless purse as my eyes adjusted to the sudden change.

She turned rapidly and held a pill bottle one inch from my nose and screamed, "What are these, you little whore?"

"Excuse me."

"What are these? Hormone pills! Hormone pills. You whore! I want to know who you've been screwing. I want to know the little bitch's name."

I felt like I was in a movie. I thought, people don't really act like this, and then I looked over at the dog. I think he felt sorry for me.

She was close enough to bite my nose. "Answer me whore boy," she screamed. Spit flew on my face like tiny cold pinpricks.

She reached back to her purse and pulled out a gun.

I heard myself say out loud, "You have a gun."

Lida said, "Yes, Barry, I have a gun. A loaded gun. Do

you think I didn't notice how uninterested you were this time? Do you think I didn't notice the difference in your kiss? You've been gone all the time, and now the hormone pills. Do you think I'm a fuckin' idiot? Do you?"

I said in a low voice, "No...but, wasn't there a rule? Some rule about being able to see other people?"

Lida walked around to the end of the bed, never moving her eyes from mine, and placed the cold barrel of the gun against the place my balls used to be.

She said, "You're gonna tell me the little bitch's name, or I'm gonna blow your balls across the room."

She glanced down, "Jesus Christ. They're gone."

She lifted up my unit and looked around like I imagine a gynecologist looks around a patient in the office. The dog moved to the end of the bed next to Lida and seemed to be trying to figure out the problem. Like a madwoman in a movie, Lida Griggs wiggled the tip of the gun barrel into the crack of my ass, looked me in the eye, and said slowly, "You better sleep with one eye open, lover. I'm not done with you."

Lida changed clothes in front of me, packed up the big purse, and walked out of my bedroom with the dog behind her. I heard the front door close, and for the second time in a relatively short stretch of my life I found myself in an odd situation. Naked, tied to my own bed, with no possible explanation on Earth, and my mother expected any minute with meatloaf and sweet tea.

My life used to be normal. At least it seemed normal. Maybe I cared too much about meaningless sexual encounters with random women. Maybe I should have gotten past that stage in my hormonal development and cared about nurturing lifelong friendships, family relationships, and other long-term goals, but I had no idea the punishment for my lust would be the permanent loss of my testicles and the horror of being discovered tied up naked in my bed with the lights on, no one else in the apartment, behind locked doors. Thank God the dog is gone, I thought. And then I heard the front door open.

"Barry, honey, time for your dinner."

CHAPTER THREE

MIGHTY MARVIN AND THE TROLL PATROL

My mother believed the ridiculous story about burglars tying me up and promising to kill me and my family if I reported the crime to the police. It's amazing what a mother is willing to believe in order to avoid facing dirty little questions about her only son. After she left that night I slept for two full days with no idea of light or dark. I woke up to the phone ringing incessantly. I finally climbed out of the smelly bed on the twenty-fifth ring.

"Barry, where the hell you been?"

It was Donald, my dumb friend. Not really a friend. More like a drinking buddy. A guy who sits at the bar with you and tells lies. The girls love him. He's handsome and dumb. One time I overheard two strange girls by the pool table call him "Dumb Donald" like they called him that all the time. They called me "the guy with Dumb Donald."

"Tonight's the night, Barry. "All you can drink and midget wrestling at Redheads. What's the matter with you?"

"What time is it?" I asked.

It didn't sound so bad. I needed to get out of the house and have a beer. Donald picked me up in his Corvette. He's been married and divorced three times. After each divorce he buries himself up to his neck in debt and upgrades his automobile. Donald actually still winks at women. I don't think this tactic has been successful for any man anywhere in the world in the past forty years, but Donald can't help himself.

We pulled into the parking lot and parked next to a van in the only available space. In fancy red letters on the side of the van it said "Mighty Marvin and the Troll Patrol: Midget Wrestling at Its Finest."

We haven't really come very far in this civilization, have we? Grown people, hundreds of them, flocking to see deformed little men fighting each other. I couldn't wait to get inside. We were lucky enough to get a table near the front. Donald brought me a drink from the bar.

"What's this?"

"Rum and Coke."

"I don't drink rum and Coke."

"What?"

"I don't drink rum and Coke."

"Look at that midget at the bar with boots," Donald pointed and said, "You think he wrestles in those boots? Maybe he's Mighty Marvin."

I drank my rum and Coke and ordered another. I felt lightheaded and almost happy. Dumb Donald winked at the girl next to us and she turned her back.

Donald leaned over and said, "Is this a gay bar?"

"I have no idea. Haven't you been here before?"

"Hell no," Donald said. "I thought you'd been here before."

We both looked around the room for familiar signs of heterosexuality. And then a man stepped into the ring with a microphone.

"Ladies and gentlemen, welcome to Redheads. Tonight's feature event will be a full-contact match between Mighty Marvin in this corner."

A small man appeared in the ring in blue tights and

laced-up blue wrestling boots. He bounced around the ring to loud applause and retreated to his corner. His face looked old and mean.

"And in this corner, Rodney and John-John, the Troll Patrol."

Two identical midgets dressed in green entered the ring. They were nasty little men with goat beards and jewelry. They taunted and cursed at Marvin in the other corner, and it become apparent, even to Donald, that we were in a gay bar. I can't be sure what triggered our recognition, but at the same time we looked at each other with the shared fear of two homophobic men preparing to watch two mean little midgets beat up one mean little midget.

"Let the games begin."

As soon as the bell rang it was like a pack of dogs let loose. Those strong little bastards were throwing each other around by the hair and pinching each other's titties until they were red like fire. I finished my second drink and ordered a third between rounds. People were screaming and throwing money in the ring. Dumb Donald was mesmerized.

Finally Mighty Marvin did a wild double dropkick and laid out the green guys side by side. The announcer entered the ring with his microphone and held the stubby arm of Marvin high in the air proclaiming victory. The green guys crawled out on their bellies with boos from the oddball crowd.

"Winner, and still undefeated, Mighty Marvin."

Dumb Donald was clapping like the town idiot, and suddenly I couldn't stop laughing.

"What's so funny?" somebody said.

It was Mighty Marvin. He had grabbed the microphone away and was pointing at me from the center of the little wrestling ring.

"What's so funny?" he screamed again.

The room grew unpleasantly quiet. I stopped laughing one second too late. The tail end of my laugh sounded like a hyena. I looked at Donald, and he was gone. His chair was empty.

"I asked you a question. What's so funny?" He said it slow and dramatic.

I looked around the room and all eyes were on me. From behind I felt a force push me from my chair toward the ring. The green midgets were on either side, and I lost my balance falling forward and literally rolling through the ringside ropes and landing in a heap at the laced blue boots of the man they called Mighty Marvin.

Surely this is a joke, I thought, and then the little bastard was stomping me. He was pulling and twisting, rolling me over, and I was in a headlock. He stunk like rotten meat.

"Stop. Stop," I yelled, but I could barely hear myself. My ears were raw and there was nothing left to do but fight back. I punched him in the gut with no success and wrenched my head free from his vice-like wooden arms. I stepped back a few feet to catch my breath, and the creature barreled at my midsection, bent over at a full gallop. His force knocked us both over the ropes and out of the ring where the back of my head slammed into the edge of a table. My finger somehow found itself in his mouth and he bit down.

"Jesus Christ," I yelled. "Are you out of your mind?"

I ran. I got up and just ran, one hand on the back of my bleeding head and the other hand throbbing in pain with little teeth marks on the thumb. When I was out the door and down the steps I spotted the van across the parking lot as I heard the door slam behind. I turned to see all three of the crazy little sons-of-bitches coming after me.

"What's so funny?" Marvin kept screaming. "What's so funny?"

"Nothing," I yelled. "Leave me alone."

I ran toward the van wondering if Donald's car on the far side would be unlocked. When I turned the corner around the back of the van I was horrified to see an empty parking space. Donald was gone. Gone away from this place, and I was tackled with such brutal force my face hit the pavement before I could lift my hands.

One of the green guys opened the back doors of the van while the other two lifted me up and pushed me inside. Before I could get my bearings Marvin was driving out the parking lot while the green guys sat down on homemade benches on either side of me as I lay in the middle of the van. My face burned, and the hair on the back of my head felt thick.

A light came on in the van, a single bulb hanging from a wire on the ceiling above me. I could see porno magazines and empty beer cans. There were clothes piled up next to a box of chicken bones, a loaf of bread, empty whiskey bottles, a chainsaw, and one Fig Newton stuck to the floor a few inches from my eye. I thought, this couldn't possibly be happening. It's not possible that I've been kidnaped by midgets who just beat me up in a gay bar. I thought about those television cop shows that say you should listen for noises when you are locked in the trunk of a car to get an idea where you're being taken. Factories, trains, church clocks, whatever. My senses began to heighten.

One of the green midgets said, "Where you wanna go?" as he thumbed through a *Playboy* magazine.

"What?"

"Where you wanna go? We'll drop you off."

I was silent for a moment and then said, "What do you mean?"

Marvin laughed up front and said, "We ain't gonna kill you. It's all part of the show."

"What show?" I asked.

The green guy said, "We had to make a quick exit, if you know what I mean?"

"No, I don't know what you mean. And I don't want to know. Why don't you just take me to the hospital."

Marvin spoke up, "Don't even think about going to the cops. They'll laugh your ass out the station."

He was right. We rode in silence. One green midget snored while the other seemed to actually be reading an article in his magazine. The van came to a stop and Marvin said, "Welcome to the hospital."

Every bone in my body ached as I lifted myself up off the sticky floor of the van and let myself out. Marvin drove away, and the last thing I saw was his puffy little hand waving goodbye out the open window.

CHAPTER FOUR

LONNIE GREEN AND NEWTON CREECH

I finally made it home from the hospital in the early morning hours in the backseat of a taxicab. Home is apartment C-2 of the St. Charles Guest House on Prytania Street in the Garden District of New Orleans, "The City That Care Forgot." Maybe that explains a few things. I am a semipermanent resident in a small hotel where people come and go. My apartment consists of three rooms: a bedroom, a bathroom, and a living room. It is situated at the top of a flight of stairs at the beginning of a long indoor hallway. The knowledge that I had to wake up for work in just a few hours kept me from falling asleep at all. The red numbers on the clock by the bed seemed to glow like the lights of a fire engine.

I began to formulate a plan to ask my boss for a leave of absence. I had no vacation days, or sick days, or any other days left to take, and my crusty old boss was beginning to figure out the huge amount of energy I expended for the sole purpose of accomplishing nothing. Selling insurance was boring, and in my twelve months in the business I actually succeeded at making it more boring. My plan was the same every day. When the boss had walked past my door three times, I would leave the office for "a meeting." I returned in time to be seen once more before lunch. After lunch I worked thirty minutes in a row, read the newspaper folded inside a file, and stared at the clock.

I arrived at the office with a shaved spot on the back

of my head where the doctor inserted the five stitches. The teeth marks on my finger were still visible around the Band-Aid, and my groin ached with a slow hum.

The young receptionist, Lucy, was in her usual spot when I walked through the front door. She wears inappropriate clothing daily and is a reliable source of inspiration. During her first week of employment I seized the advantage of my age and seemingly important position to ask her to dinner. It didn't go well. I'm not completely sure why. I lost patience and tried to kiss her in mid-sentence. The next day a copy of the office handbook appeared on my desk turned to section 3.7(a) concerning interoffice personal relationships. I didn't notice anything in the handbook forbidding raw and blatant lust for a co-worker and therefore continued the practice.

Which leads me to a new topic. Since the incident I have closely monitored the ebb and flow of my sexual desire. Mostly it has ebbed, but a few times it has flowed. I hold hope, but I have found my mind drifting away from the island of pure lust to a strange place. If I try too hard to figure it out I'm afraid I'll step across some ancient line and never return to the freedom of blind desire.

My office has no windows. I hadn't really noticed before. At thirty-three years old, with a college degree, I had an office with no windows. My walls were mostly bare. I had a certificate from a seminar in North Carolina framed behind my desk. My mother gave me one of those brass lamps with the green glass top. It sat on the corner of the desk next to a wooden nameplate. As I stood at the door to my office on this particular morning there was a distinct sadness, almost like a smell.

I walked down the hall to the office of the boss, Mr. Lonnie Green, the king of insurance. The hallway walls are lined with plaques and diplomas for every conceivable award and training school known to man. Lonnie has won them all. He can sell insurance standing on his head naked in a room full of nuns.

Lonnie's door was open. He was on the telephone leaning back in his special chair from Hong Kong. He loved to tell the story of that stupid chair. It was a gift from the ambassador of China. I can't remember the rest of the story. I sat in the chair once. It had the odor of stale farts trapped forever in fabric.

Lonnie waved his hand for me to enter. I sat down across the desk and tried not to listen to his conversation or look at the walls of achievement. He had a habit in this situation of staring directly at the person in his office as he spoke directly to the person on the phone. Subliminally I imagine he was saying, "Barry, this is how you make a sale. Son, watch me and learn, and one day you too may be sitting in a chair like mine, surrounded by the souvenirs of success."

Lonnie hung up the phone, swivelled in his chair to face me, and didn't say a word. He waited for me to start.

"Mr. Green, I've got a family emergency. I was hoping to take a leave of absence for a few months. Get everything in order."

There was a pause, long and unpleasant. Lonnie Green studied the scratches on my face and the Band-Aid on my finger. He finally spoke.

"First of all, Barry, you're lying. I've spent forty years in this business, and I know the difference. You don't have a family emergency, and I doubt seriously you'd even know what the hell a family emergency looks like.

"You're lazy, Barry. You get paid to fold up newspapers in a file and read 'em on the job. You walk around Lucy's desk like a four-balled tomcat on a Saturday night. You go to meetings that don't exist, and the worst part of it all, the worst part is you don't even care enough to cover it up."

We sat across the desk from each other for a moment. He was right. I didn't like him much, but he was right.

And then Lonnie said something odd. "I don't think men should wear makeup."

It was quiet again. There was nothing to say. I would have preferred the man to fire me, but we just sat there, staring at each other. I stood up slowly and walked away from Lonnie's desk.

From behind me I heard the man say, "You've got a big freakin' knot on the back of your head. Did somebody whack you upside the skull with a Tombigbee stick?"

I don't know what that means. I can't answer a question I don't understand. I just kept walking out the door, down the hall, and straight to the bathroom mirror. Makeup? What makeup? Is the world so full of freaks that I can't even have normal conversations? Somehow, has the loss of my testicles changed the way my brain processes words?

Thank God it was Friday. When I got home that afternoon I barricaded myself inside, unplugged the phone, and turned up the air-conditioning. I vowed only to leave the bed in case of emergency. But then again, according to Lonnie, I'm probably not capable of recognizing an emergency. What exactly does that mean?

I slept very little during those two days and nights. Mostly I thought about things. The world had taken an ugly turn. Just a few weeks earlier I would have said I was happy. Then, rolled up in a ball under the covers in my freezing lonely room, I wondered what I'd been doing the last fifteen years. Besides my mother, there wasn't even anyone to call. My only friend, Donald, left me to die in a gay bar. My "girlfriend" threatened to kill me. And my boss thinks I wear makeup.

And then it dawned on me. I will never have a child. Ever. The thought rose slowly to the surface of my mind and rested on top of everything else. I will never have a child. I will end with me, a victim of my own victim.

It never seemed important before. I'd answered the questions of every nosy aunt and uncle, grandparent, and family friend. When you're thirty-three with no prospects for marriage, old people worry.

"No thank you. Marriage is outdated. And children. They smell, and then they grow up to hate you and take your money."

Those words were easy to speak when the option remained. But now no option remained. A door had been closed. Not just closed, but removed, filled in and covered over, as if no door ever existed.

And then fate reached out and whacked me in the back of the head with a Tombigbee stick. I called in sick that Monday. A man in a uniform knocked on my door to deliver a letter. I signed where he told me to sign and crawled back inside my frozen cave. Sitting on the couch I opened this letter dated July twenty-first.

Mr. Barry Munday
St. Charles Guest House, Room C-2
New Orleans, Louisiana

Dear Mr. Munday:

I have been retained to represent the interests of Ms. Ginger Farley. Ms. Farley believes that you are the father of her unborn child conceived on or about February 11th. I have been retained by my client for the purpose of pursuing all legal action necessary to establish paternity and obtain a child support order consistent with Rule 32 of the Louisiana Rules of Judicial Administration.

If you wish to admit paternity prior to the birth of the child I can draft all necessary documentation to be signed by both parties and filed at the appropriate time. If you wish to deny paternity I will seek an order of the Court for DNA testing, and a hearing will take place for the Court to make a judicial finding concerning the issue of paternity.

Please contact me with your response within ten (10) days of the date of this letter. If no communication has been received by my office within ten (10) days, I will assume you are denying paternity and then proceed accordingly.

Sincerely,

Newton Creech
Attorney at Law

I actually read the letter from top to bottom six times without stopping. The name Ginger Farley rang no bells whatsoever. February 11th meant nothing to me. Before the incident I would have known how I was expected to react. Under my new circumstances, I had no idea. I was confused by the exhilaration.

I picked up the phone and called the law office of Newton Creech.

"May I speak to Mr. Creech, please?"

"May I ask who's calling?"

"Barry Munday."

"And Mr. Munday, what does this concern?"

I hesitated, "Ginger Farley."

"Oh," the voice said, "I understand."

I was placed on hold where I listened to Bob Marley sing "I Shot the Sheriff." And then a man's voice said, "Mr. Munday, Newton Creech here."

"Ah...yes, sir. I got your letter today. Just had a few questions."

"Mr. Munday, I can't give you legal advice, but I'll answer the questions the best I can."

I sat at my little table with the letter and a calendar opened in front of me.

"Well, first off, how does this Ginger Farley know that I'm the father of this baby? How does she know?"

Newton Creech said, "That's an easy question. Ms. Farley has had intercourse one time in her entire life. With you. On February 11th of this year. It wasn't hard for her to figure it out."

"Wow," I said, "O.K."

"Do you have another question, Mr. Munday?"

"Yeah, I do. Where did we meet, me and Ms. Farley?"

The man's voice changed. "Let's not play games, Barry. If you want to play games, go hire a lawyer."

"I'm not playing games, sir. I just want to make sure this is my baby. I'll take a blood test voluntarily. Can we do the test before the baby is born?"

"We can," the lawyer said. "It's more complicated and expensive, but we can do it. I'll make the arrangements, and my office will be in touch."

"Hey," I said, "could I meet Ginger Farley? Maybe have a cup of coffee or something?"

There was silence. "Do you really have no recollection of your sexual encounter with Ms. Farley? None? Because I find that hard to believe."

I didn't answer.

"Anyway," he continued, "I'll tell her you'd like to meet her somewhere and she can call you. How's that?"

"O.K.," I answered. And we hung up.

A baby, maybe my baby, inside a complete stranger, conceived at random before I lost my testicles to a madman in a movie theater. Sitting in my underwear wrapped in a blanket at the little table on a haphazard Monday afternoon I saw my life take a slow turn like a giant ship in the ocean changing directions.

CHAPTER FIVE

GINGER FARLEY

Two days later, sitting at my desk reading "Dear Abby," Lucy buzzed.

"Line one, a lady named Ginger Farley. Good luck."

And then she hung up. Why would she say "good luck"?

I picked up the phone and pressed line one.

"Hello," I said.

There was silence.

"Hello. Is this Ginger? Hello."

In the background I could hear a television, and what sounded like a blender, and then a voice came on the line.

"Hello."

"Hello," I said again.

"Is this Barry?"

"Yes, it is," I said. "I was hoping you'd call."

"Don't be a turd, Barry," she said. "A turd is a person who says things they don't mean. You've been doing that your whole life, Barry, but you're not gonna do it with me."

Her voice was dedicated to the message, but she seemed distracted. I could hear the blender still running in the background.

"Are you busy?" I said. "Maybe I could call you back later?"

"Am I busy?" she asked.

The blender cut off, and I heard what sounded like a toilet flush. Then she said, "I just held the phone in the commode so you could hear the sound of my waste products leaving the universe of my house."

There was a pause, and then she said, "My lawyer says you're mentally ill, and I should only meet you in a public place."

"What?"

"My lawyer says you have some sort of mental illness. Don't you think you should've let me know something before we conceived a child together?"

Her phone fell to the floor and bounced like a rock against my ear. The blender came back to life, and from far away I heard her say, "I'll meet you at 6:30 at Redheads."

Before I could answer there was a dial tone. I remembered that Redheads was the bar with the midgets. How could I go back there? Was it just a coincidence? What kind of a woman was I dealing with?

In my history with women I have noticed a disturbing trend. I have a pattern of attraction to women who are mentally unbalanced, like Lida, for example. The unbalance actually acts initially as an aphrodisiac, like froth on the top of a dark beer. Then later, sometimes quickly, the mental unbalance is no longer a good thing. It becomes a bad thing. Very bad.

I searched the recesses of my memory the rest of the afternoon for any hint of Ginger Farley. Perhaps she used a different name. Perhaps I shouldn't drink so much. I held hope that the sight of her face would jumpstart a long line of recollections. I can't lie, I also held hope that Ginger Farley was a beautiful woman, tight and tan, with slender legs and attentive breasts.

I got to Redheads early and found a seat at a table facing the door. The place wasn't crowded. I ordered a Coke and waited. I watched a blonde in a red dress come through the glass door and look around the room. My heart stopped, and then she waved to a friend and sat down at another table. From 6:15 to 6:45 seven or eight women walked in the place alone. They ranged from a college girl to a three-hundred-pound woman with a briefcase. And then, at nearly seven, a strange little woman entered the bar and walked directly to my table. She sat down.

It was obvious this woman recognized me. She was short, mid-twenties, dressed with an odd, artsy flair, round eyeglasses, ugly black shoes, and tiny white hands. At first glance there was absolutely nothing about the woman attractive other than the hint of mental instability.

"What did you want to see me for, Barry?"

I searched her face for clues. Before I could answer her question a large man stepped out of a back room in my field of vision. It was the man who had stood in the midget wrestling ring with the microphone. He looked straight at me and then was standing at our table almost instantly.

"Aren't you the son-of-a-bitch who got in a fight with the midget and skipped out on the bar tab?"

I stammered, "Well...it wasn't really a fight, and there wasn't a bar tab."

"Bullshit. You and your buddy left owing twenty-five bucks, and them damn midgets skipped on a two-hundred-dollar tab. You're gonna pay all of it, today, or you're gonna wish you did."

Ginger had a look of amusement as she tilted her face back and forth from the man's face to mine like a tennis match.

"Wait a minute," I said, "why should I pay the midget tab? I don't even know those guys."

"Really," the man said. "You left that night in their van. I ain't gonna argue about it. You pay it, or leave here in the back of a cop car," he hesitated, "or an ambulance."

It occurred to me the man was gay. It also occurred to me that he had a point. I pulled out my wallet and handed him a credit card. Ginger and I were left alone again. Thirty seconds earlier I was sure the situation couldn't possibly be less comfortable. I was wrong.

Ginger said, "You know, I hope babies can't understand English in the womb. I'd hate to think this child, before it can even be born, would have the misfortune of hearing that last conversation."

"How far along are you?" I asked.

"Well, on February 11th, a few minutes before midnight, your little sperm army stormed the pink beach. You count the days."

She was a bitter toad, but behind the glasses I could see she had eyes. There was a constant feeling that she had somewhere else to be. The same distraction I felt on the phone.

"Ginger, I don't want to offend you, but I've just got to know, are you absolutely, one hundred percent sure the baby is mine?"

Without a change of expression she said, "You little shit-eater, I'm weak one night, one night, and with a little shit-eater like you. God knows why, at least I hope He does, and now you want to sit here in your midget bar and ask me crap.

"Yes, Barry, this baby is yours, and you're not gonna weasel away from the responsibility. You're gonna stand up like the man you're not and take this obligation square in the chest, or my lawyer's gonna ram it so far up your tight ass you'll think the devil got lucky."

She paused, "Is there any part of this you don't understand?"

I can't explain why, but as she spoke I thought about that baby, my baby, inside this crazy woman across the table, just below the skin of her belly, rolling around in the warmth, and I smiled.

"Is this funny to you?" she asked.

"No, Ginger, it's not funny, it's a miracle. You just don't know. Can I touch it?"

"Touch what?" she winced.

"Touch your belly. Touch where the baby is. Can I just put my hand on it?"

"Shit, no. You've done all the touchin' you're gonna do."

"Please. Let me touch it. It's not just yours, you know. It's mine too."

Believe me, I know my words and actions were out of character. I know it now, and I knew it then, but for the first time in my life I felt a gentle current pull me somewhere. All the fractured pieces of my existence seemed to drift into place.

"Please."

Her beady eyes peered over the top of her round glasses, and I was given unspoken permission. I scooted my chair to her side of the table and wiped the sweat from my palm on the thigh of my blue jeans.

Ginger lifted the loose shirt from her side and I slid my hand underneath. Her skin was warm and tight over a bulge. I had a desire to place my face against her belly, and I knelt down next to her, and placed my face next to my hand on the belly of the mother of my child. I closed my eyes and smelled the skin. It was religious. Strange and religious, and I haven't been to church since I was a boy. I felt the emergence of my first erection since the incident.

I was startled by a man's voice. "You're a nasty son-of-a-bitch, aren't you?"

I pulled my head from its secret place to see the man standing with my credit card and bill.

"After you sign this," he said, "I'm gonna ask you to leave here and never come back."

"That's a deal," I said. I signed the credit card slip, took Ginger by the hand, and we walked outside into the New Orleans summertime thick heat. I was immediately struck by the fact that Ginger was even less attractive in full daylight. My erection died without a fight.

What is beauty anyway? During the Renaissance they sat around all day painting fat chicks. Chinese women bind their feet, and some African tribal women stretch their necks like human giraffes. All in the name of beauty. In some certain place in history, in some certain era, maybe Ginger Farley would have been worshiped for her beauty like Nefertiti. We stared at each other for a moment.

I heard myself say, "Ginger, I know this baby is mine, and I can't tell you how, I just know. We don't need a blood test. I'll just sign the papers. Let me go to the doctor with you. Let me see the baby on the X-ray thing. Do you know if it's a boy or a girl?"

Ginger looked puzzled.

"It's called a sonogram, and no, I haven't found out what it is. I don't want to know."

"Can I go to the doctor with you, please?" I asked.

She squinted and said, "I guess so. My next appointment is tomorrow."

She turned and walked away, stopped, and said, "I'll call you and let you know where to meet me, but don't get the wrong idea. You're still a shit-eater."

CHAPTER SIX

FERTILE GROUND

We sat in the waiting room of the doctor's office. Women came and went, with and without husbands, some obviously pregnant, some not. It was fertile ground for the male imagination. There was proof before my eyes that each of these ladies engaged in some sort of sexual activity. No longer a leap of faith, actual proof.

Across from us sat a very well-dressed, social woman in her thirties. There were no signs of pregnancy, and I imagined some sort of venereal disease, red and spotty, from one thigh to the other. She shifted in her chair under my watchful eye and pretended to read a magazine.

Ginger and I sat side by side on a yellow love seat without speaking. I reviewed my list of questions for the doctor. This was a whole new world, a world I hadn't even taken the time to learn about. I slowly looked around the room at the breasts of each of the women. The baby book I saw at the library had a whole chapter on the enlargement of a woman's breasts during pregnancy. There were even photographs of the handiwork of the tittie fairy. And then I felt Ginger's pointy elbow against my ribs.

"What are you lookin' at, freak? Why don't you just walk around the room and take a bite?"

It hadn't occurred to me that while I watched, someone else was watching me.

"Sorry."

A nurse stepped into the waiting room and said,

"Ginger Farley. Come on back."

I tried to walk across the room and down the hall like a man who knew what he was doing.

Ginger climbed up and sat on a table. I sat in the only chair available and removed the list from my pocket.

The nurse and Ginger chatted, and I listened. She lifted Ginger's shirt, and I was allowed to see the belly. The nurse moved a little item across Ginger's stomach and there was the pulse of a gentle heartbeat.

"It's strong," the nurse said. "Strong and clear."

"Can we see it?" I blurted out.

The nurse turned and looked at me like she didn't know I was there. I felt like a boy in the girl's locker room.

Ginger said, "I don't want to find out if it's a boy or a girl. If we do a sonogram today, will it be obvious?"

"Probably not. Just remind Suzie you don't want to know."

The nurse finished her business and turned to the door. On the way out she made a general comment, "Take off your clothes, put on the gown, and the doctor will be in to see you in just a few minutes."

I tried not to smile.

When the nurse was gone, Ginger said, "Turn around, idiot."

While I stared at the wall and listened closely to the sounds of undressing, I thought, in the past I've allowed women to treat me with such open disdain, but always, always, I only allowed the behavior in exchange for physical favors, or at least with some distant hope of touching. This was different. Ginger Farley was the most asexual human being I had ever met. I wondered how on

Earth I ever convinced this angry vegetarian to copulate.

Dr. Maury Shriver entered the room. He was a huge smile in a white coat and walked with big steps like Groucho Marx.

"Good morning, good morning."

He stuck out his hand and we shook like men. With his back to Ginger he winked at me like we shared a secret.

"Ginger girl, how you been feelin'?"

"I've got heartburn crawlin' up my throat after every meal, my feet are swollen dough balls, I pee two thousand times a day, and I haven't taken a dump since last Tuesday. Besides that, I'm the picture of health."

The doctor smiled and moved the stethoscope around from back to front. He looked at a chart and said, "O.K., we've got a due date of December 7th." He turned to me and explained, "Most people think the gestation period is only nine months. Actually, we count those nine months from the day of the first missed period. So really, the gestation period from the date of conception is closer to nine and a half or ten months."

I wondered if all gynecologists are so happy. Too much knowledge can be a dangerous thing. When I was a teenager I got a job at my favorite restaurant. After two weeks I never ate there again.

I spoke up. "Dr. Shriver, I just wanted to ask a few questions if I could. I'm Barry Munday. I'm the father."

"O.K., Barry Munday, ask away."

I looked down at my list.

(#1) "Will I be allowed in the delivery room? I want to be the first person to touch the baby when it gets out."

I expected a snide remark from Ginger but none came.

"Absolutely, Barry Munday. We'll be side-by-side. Watch your videos and go to the classes."

(#2) "Are there any foods Ginger shouldn't eat? I read somewhere that pregnant women shouldn't eat blue cheese."

Ginger closed her eyes and said, "Are you retarded?"

Dr. Shriver kept on smiling. He said, "I've never heard the one about blue cheese. We've already given Ginger a book about diet and exercise." He checked his watch.

I didn't want Ginger to hear the third question. I leaned toward the doctor and whispered, "Is it O.K. for her to have sex while she's pregnant?"

The doctor put his face close to mine and said, "Good luck, son." And then he was gone like a tall, happy Groucho Marx.

Suzie the nurse appeared at the door. She walked us down to the sonogram room. I was directed to a certain chair next to a metal table. Ginger was positioned face up with her legs dangling over the edge. Before I could pay proper attention, Ginger's gown was pulled up just below her breasts and a white sheet was wrapped around her lower half. The edge of the sheet was below the bellybutton and just above the pubic region.

The nurse put some clear jelly on Ginger's stomach and pressed against the skin with something in her hand. On the screen, in black and white, there was a form. I stood from my chair for a better view. There was a head, and legs, and skeleton ribs. The nurse rubbed around several times before finding the right spot. Her efforts pushed the white sheet a few inches south, revealing seven or eight delightful brown pubic hairs. To my surprise my eyes went back to the black-and-white screen.

And then it moved. The little hand reached up and *what stage?* rubbed the little face, and I could see the fingers. I could count the individual fingers. Five. One, two, three, four, five.

I felt dizzy and my breathing changed. Sweat appeared on my forehead in a split second and the nurse said, "Sir, are you O.K.? Do you need to sit down?"

"Yes. I do."

Ginger had that same odd look of amusement. I sat in my little chair and put my head between my legs like a man preparing for a plane to crash.

It was real. I knew it was real anyway, but seeing that alien baby on the screen, scratching its little head like a person was more reality than I expected.

Ginger said to the nurse, "That idiot told the doctor he wanted to help deliver the baby. He sees a sonogram and hyperventilates. Maybe he could wear a football helmet in the delivery room so when he faints nobody will have to stop and tend to him." They laughed.

I could feel the coldness of my face resting on my arm. Suzie went away and came back with Ginger's clothes. I could hear her get dressed behind a curtain. The nurse handed me a picture. It was a picture of the baby taken at the exact moment it held up its hand, with the fingers spread like a star.

I haven't cried since my dog died during my junior year in high school, but holding that picture in my hand I felt emotion rise inside me from my chest up to my eyes.

I walked out of the office with Ginger, and we rode the elevator down to the bottom floor. We were silent until we reached her car in the parking lot.

Ginger said, "Don't ask me why, but my parents want to meet you. They want you to come to dinner tomorrow night."

Before I could answer she said, "I know it's stupid. It's not my idea. If you don't wanna go, I'll just tell 'em you don't wanna go. That'll be the end of it."

"I'll go," I said.

She seemed puzzled again. Ginger said, "My parents won't like you."

"Why not?"

"They just won't. I'll call you tomorrow."

And then she was gone. I sat in my car and looked at the picture of the baby. I looked at every blurry black-and-white detail. Something was happening to me.

CHAPTER SEVEN

AN EVENING WITH THE FARLEYS

Ginger Farley picked me up in her little green car to go to the house of her parents for dinner. I was nervous. Very nervous. I'd met parents before, but certainly never in a situation such as this.

"Ginger, can you give me an idea of what to expect?"

"Not really."

"Are your parents mad?"

"Yes, I think so."

She just drove along offering nothing. Finally, we pulled up in the driveway of a house the size of a mansion. I hadn't paid attention to the direction we traveled, but now I could see we were in the fancy section of the Garden District off St. Charles Avenue, a beautiful area of the city far removed from the tourist traps and street performers in the French Quarter.

I began to consider the possibility of running away. The thought of the next several hours was indigestible. It was clear I could expect no help from Ginger. We walked to the front door together, and she pressed the doorbell.

Ginger turned calmly to me and said, "My mother and father believe that you put drugs in my drink and had intercourse with me while I was unconscious."

I stared into her face for any hint of humor. The words in her sentence came together in my mind, and I heard myself utter a noise. The door opened, and I stood before the mother of Ginger Farley, a perfect replica of the daughter, except elegantly dressed. The chance to run had passed.

There were introductions I cannot recall. Mr. Farley requested that we speak alone in the library before dinner. He was a large man, not fat, with a big sturdy face. I followed him into a room, and we closed the door. He sat down behind a huge mahogany desk and motioned for me to sit on the other side. I still held some distant hope that nasty Ginger had played a joke.

"Well, Mr. Munday, we've got ourselves a situation here. Don't we?"

I was silent.

He continued, "I suppose I've got several choices. I can take you in the backyard and beat the living shit outta you."

He waited for a response. None was forthcoming.

"Or, I can call my friend at the police station, have you charged with rape, and put your sorry ass in jail."

So far there were no good choices.

"Or, I can make damn sure you accept the responsibility of being a father, every day, of every week, for the rest of your life. Financially, morally, spiritually, with a dedication that I'm sure a shit-eater like you has never fathomed."

I knew now where lovely Ginger got her vocabulary. There was a long pause before I started to speak.

The big man said, "Before you say a word, one word, you need to know that the choice I make depends completely on the next five minutes of this conversation. I hope you have no doubt, none whatsoever, that I have the means to accomplish any of these choices."

I closed my eyes and spoke slowly, "I'm not sure, Mr.

Farley, exactly what you've been told."

He leaned forward in his chair and said, "Then you tell me, Mr. Barry Munday, your version of events."

It occurred to me that I had no version of events. I had no recollection at all of his daughter or the conception of our child. I could not dispute anything. I couldn't imagine a judge would accept the excuse of drinking too much or losing track of my casual sexual encounters, and I was damn sure the man across the desk wouldn't take very well to such an explanation.

There was a knock on the library door, and a young woman stepped inside. She was gorgeous.

"Daddy, it's time for dinner," she said.

I was saved.

The young woman turned to me and said, "You must be Barry the rapist. I'm Ginger's little sister, Jennifer," she smiled.

I got up quickly to follow her out in the wake of her interruption.

Mr. Farley said, "Sit down."

I sat down. The word "rapist" swam around my brain.

"Barry, we're gonna leave this room with an understanding. You'll do exactly what I tell you to do, when I tell you to do it, or your life as you know it will be over."

I just wanted out of there. I would've sold my soul to the devil for a pack of chewing gum if I could just go home.

"Yes, sir."

I had the feeling I wasn't the first person to sit across the desk from Tom Farley and accept his terms without exception. We stood and walked out together to the dining room.

My place at the table was next to Ginger, who offered me no reassurance. Jennifer sat directly across from me and obviously believed the entire situation was funny. The room was so thick with discomfort I could barely eat. I remember small talk, but mostly I remember the first touch of Jennifer's bare foot on my leg under the table. It started at the ankle on the inside of my right leg and crept gently up to the knee. She talked and giggled incessantly about college and boyfriends and football games at L.S.U. Her toes wedged under my pants leg until they touched bare skin, and God help me, I felt the beginning of a secret erection below the white napkin in my lap. I tried to concentrate on my only ally in the room, the unborn baby resting in the womb of the belligerent toad in the chair next to me.

"Tell us about yourself, Barry," Mrs. Farley said quietly, and without conviction.

I imagined Jennifer's toenails were painted red, and her feet were creamy white perfection.

"There isn't much to tell, Mrs. Farley. I work at Lonnie Green's insurance agency on Constance Street. I've been there for almost a year."

"Really," Mr. Farley said, "Lonnie Green is a friend of mine. Maybe I could stop by and the three of us could go to lunch."

I wanted to say, "Mr. Farley, your daughter has her naked creamy white foot wedged between my thighs. I don't care if you know Lonnie Green. And I didn't rape your frog-like daughter. This baby is my baby, and you don't have to threaten me with violence or criminal prosecution for me to accept the responsibility of fatherhood. You don't understand, and neither does anyone else at this table, that this baby is a miracle, a guaranteed genuine miracle that has nothing to do with you, or Lonnie Green, or even Ginger Farley."

Instead I said, "O.K."

The situation was so utterly out of control I don't think it would've mattered what I said. My life was spinning in space like a planet with no axis. I began to see little spots in my field of vision, white sparkles on the edges. What could possibly happen next? I excused myself to the bathroom, which I had noticed down the long hall across from the library door.

My bowels picked a fine time to move, but move they did. I was in no hurry to get back to the family dinner and took my sweet time with my business. It was a luxury to be alone a few minutes to gather my thoughts. I had no idea of the trouble to come.

Tucking in my shirt I reached over and flushed the toilet. In horror I watched as the water rose, floating my turds to the surface. There was nothing to do but stand there as the turds were carried by the current to the edge of the commode, swirling nasty bits splashing down to the white tile floor. Brownish water continued to cascade down the bowl, running along the cracks in every direction.

In a panic I removed the lid to the back tank and tried to stop the rush of water. I finally got down on my knees to turn the shut-off valve closed and bring the flow to a stop. It was only a temporary victory. I felt the knees of my khaki slacks soaked in turd water. I immediately dry-heaved loudly. The smell was unbearable. I had been in the bathroom far too long. Water had made its way to the door and under the crack.

I took off my shoes and pants and stood at the big marble sink looking in the huge mirror. I placed the knees of my pants under the sink for a quick wash and promptly dry-heaved again. The harder I scrubbed, the worse it smelled. I located a hair dryer, plugged it in, and started the loud drying process. There was a mess on the floor, and then I noticed the window.

There was a loud bang on the door. Mr. Farley yelled, "What the hell's goin' on in there? There's water out here."

I turned off the hair dryer. I could hear the whispers of Mrs. Farley and Jennifer outside the door. There was brown water all around my socked feet. Wet toilet paper hung around the rim of the commode. The room smelled like a port-o-let, and I stood looking in the mirror at myself in my underpants.

The next thing I knew I was crawling headfirst out the window into a holly bush. There was no plan, only the undeniable instinct to run. I heard the man beat on the door again. The bark of a dog in the dark came from my right, so I ran in my wet socked feet to the left. I jumped over the side fence, caught a glimpse of Ginger's car parked in the driveway, and made a quick decision. I climbed in the backseat of her car, got down low on the floorboard, and covered myself with newspapers and other debris from the backseat of the car.

It felt like a long time passed. My hearing was keen for the sound of the front door opening or closing, or voices. Finally I heard the front door of the house shut softly, footsteps down the driveway, and the car door opened. The car cranked on the first turn, and I felt movement. I couldn't be sure who was behind the wheel. Maybe Mr. Farley was driving around looking for me.

After a few minutes the car hit the open road, and once again I was reduced to listening for clues to my direction.

Ginger's voice said, "You know what? I thought I was a strange person, I thought I was a freak, but I believe you're the biggest freak I've ever known."

She continued, "I know you can hear me back there. You actually crawled out my parents' bathroom window in the middle of dinner with no pants and left behind a carnival of shit. You left your shoes, your wallet, and crawled out the window."

I heard the thud of what sounded like my wallet tossed onto the backseat above my head. Ginger started to laugh. I'd never heard her laugh before. It was actually pleasant, but she couldn't stop. There would be a moment of silence, and she would start back laughing again.

Finally I said from my hiding place on the floorboard, "Please, just take me home."

So what happened with the father?

CHAPTER EIGHT

A COMMON FEMALE COSMIC PLATEAU

When a grown man crawls through a bathroom window in his underwear, there are several ways to handle the problem. I prefer to pretend it never occurred, and move forward.

My strange enthusiasm about the baby almost immediately began spilling over into other compartments of my life. I started arriving at work earlier and actually selling people insurance policies. I began jogging, eating vegetables, and ignoring alcohol. I never really liked alcohol in the first place. It was always just a necessary part of the uniform. My kind of woman hangs around in a bar, and alcohol has been my great ally in the war on women. Unfortunately, this ally seems to have turned against me and clouded my memory. But maybe it's best I don't remember my moment of glory with Ginger Farley so many months ago. It seems more like a miracle when there are no crunchy little details. Details lead to analysis, analysis leads to reason, and reason can screw up a miracle like nothing else I know.

As we drifted slowly into the last trimester, it became apparent I would need to tell my mother the big news. I am an only child, and my father doesn't exist. My mother, not-so-secretly, has pined for a grandchild. I'm sure her sweet dreams have not included the face of Ginger Farley or the drunken immaculate conception. But after one of her evening cocktails, and the chance to envision a tiny pink baby wrapped in soft white sheets, I believed Mother would tap her unlimited resources of motherhood and embrace the thought of a grandchild in this world.

My plan included inviting Ginger to my mother's house to deliver the news. I figured it would be better to knock the whole damn thing out with one swift blow. I'd hate to go through the anxiety of delivering the news alone, and then follow up the trauma with my mother actually meeting Ginger Farley on a separate occasion. Besides, I thought, who knows, maybe my mother and Ginger would come together on some common female cosmic plateau that I couldn't possibly understand, nor want to. But then again, my gentle thoughts tend to end in violence.

I drove to Ginger's apartment in my bright red sports car. I have no idea how a car works. It seems impossible for man, any man, or woman for that matter, to build an engine out of the Earth, pour in a gallon of dinosaur juice, bolt together a few rubber wheels on each side, and then make it all move along together on command. Like I said, my car is red.

Ginger reluctantly accepted my invitation to meet my mother. Oddly, ever since the "bathroom incident" at her parents' house, she seemed to like me more. She wouldn't admit it, but we were developing some bizarre subterranean bond.

I knocked on her door, and she opened it. I was immediately struck by the ugliness of her clothes. A person doesn't consistently wear ugly clothes by accident. If a person doesn't care, they tend to lean toward comfortable clothes. But ugly clothes are a choice. Ginger Farley, for whatever warped motivation, chose to wear ugly clothes, and on this particular occasion, again with unknown motivation, she chose to wear the ugliest brown dress I had ever seen in my life, counting magazines. It's like a psychological cinnamon roll, layer on top of layer with little nuts trapped between the layers, and the center is always soft and vulnerable. I think she decided a long time ago she could never compete physically with certain women, maybe her sister, and as a backlash against the futility, Ginger Farley chose to make a statement. Her statement, loud and clear, says: "I won't compete."

"Ginger, I don't want you to take this the wrong way, but your dress doesn't do you justice."

You see, if you're going to deal with women, you've got to learn to wrap negative comments inside subtle little compliments. It works like a concussion grenade. They're usually confused and disoriented, easy to steer in the right direction.

"That's interesting, Barry. You didn't seem to have a problem with this dress the night you pulled it off."

We stood at the door, face to face. I toyed with the idea of making another comment before I turned to walk back to my red car parked on the street. She was like a dog, among other dogs, but unable to hear the sound of the special dog whistle.

We rode in silence toward my mother's modest little house. Our moments of silence were no longer uncomfortable. In fact, it was a relief not to be worried about the next thing to say. I found myself looking at her white feet stuffed inside a pair of leather sandals on the floorboard. Ginger was staring out the side window so I had a really good chance to see those feet. Unpainted toenails, short, wide, unhappy feet, crammed toe against toe. I looked up from the feet, back to the road, and to the feet again. I lifted my eyes to see Ginger watching me.

With no expression she said, "Would you like to smell 'em?"

I pretended to be concentrating on the traffic. After a few moments I said, "Why don't you paint your toenails, red or something?"

Again, with no expression, she said, "Why don't you climb up my ass with a little tiny ladder."

I had never heard that expression before.

Standing at my mother's front door, I suddenly thought about the bombshell Ginger Farley dropped on me while we were standing at the door of her parents. The words rang back to me, "My mother and father believe that you put drugs in my drink and had intercourse with me while I was unconscious." I realized that I didn't know if she meant "mistaken belief," or if Ginger had told them a lie to explain away her premarital sex, or if indeed I allowed my lust to get the best of me and made love to a sleeping cretin in a brown dress.

I wanted to say, "What difference does it make? We're all here now, and there's a baby on the way. Let's think about the baby, and the future. Tomorrow is a new day."

Instead, I just knocked on the door. In my mother's eyes I could see instant recognition of the ugly dress and the bulge underneath. I could also see that Mother had chosen to have her cocktail early that night in anticipation of the rare occasion of my inviting a girl home for dinner. Through the evening the women were involved in some type of duel with glances and comments. I imagined it was comparable to the conversation I had with Mr. Farley in his library, but with no direct confrontation.

There were several comments made throughout the night that left a lasting impression on all of us. I asked my mother to sit down in her favorite chair. She sat, petite and proper, with her thin little ankles crossed and her hands folded neatly in her lap.

"Mom. I've got something to tell you."

Ginger sat on the couch across the coffee table from me and my mother. Her knees were a few inches apart, and I caught a sideways glimpse of white panties in the valley.

"Mom, you may have noticed, Ginger's pregnant. We're gonna have a baby."

My mother stared blankly at me, waiting for something more.

I said, "A baby, mom, a baby."

She looked around the room for a familiar face and said, "Who's Ginger?"

Ginger raised her hand slowly. My mother said clearly, "I can see your panties."

Ginger leaned forward and tilted her head down to see for herself. My mother said, "Oh my God, did I say that?" She paused. "Let's eat. I'm starving. Who'd like a gin and tonic? Fresh lime?"

My mother stood and walked directly to the bedroom and stayed for thirty minutes. I left her alone and hoped the gin and estrogen would combine, boil, digest the poison, and leave behind the mother I've always known.

The buzzer on the oven went off, and my mother came out to the kitchen brand new. She gave me a hug, and hugged Ginger, before she fixed us all a drink, and we sat down at the small table together.

There was chit-chat. My mother said, "I'd like to help somehow. You two are going to need a baby bed, bottles, sheets, and lots and lots of diapers."

Chewing her roast beef Ginger said, "My baby won't wear diapers. Do you have any idea the psychological effect on a child caused by binding the child's genitalia? It's wrong."

My mother listened to the girl across the table like she was a talking monkey. I could see that my hope of Ginger Farley and my mother connecting on some universal female plateau was misguided. There would be no such connection.

Still chewing her roast beef, Ginger said, "Why is it we can teach a kitten, just a few months old, to use a sandbox, but a child, infinitely more intelligent than a kitten, walks around for two years shittin' in their pants? Why is that? I wish you'd tell me."

My mother was hypnotized. Her food grew cold on the plate. As Ginger excused herself to the bathroom and left us alone at the table, I heard my mother say to herself, "Crazy talk."

"I know what you're thinking, Mother, but she comes from a really nice family. They have a huge house off St. Charles in the Garden District. I've been there. Her sister goes to L.S.U."

My mother said nicely, "I don't care if she's a Kennedy, that girl's socially retarded. Cat box. She's gonna teach your baby to use a cat box. Can you imagine?"

I thought a moment and smiled. "No," I said. Ginger came back and sat down.

Trouble formed on the horizon like a storm across Lake Pontchartrain when I heard my dear old mother pour her third gin and tonic. One drink dulls her edges, two makes her flighty and funny. Three is trouble. Unpredictable, loose, silver-tongued trouble.

Ginger insisted we stay for desert. She seemed to sense the danger and wallow in the possibility. I ate my bread pudding in large bites. Ginger slowly nibbled and stirred the conversation. Right when I thought there was a chance at escape, my mother said with raised eyebrows, "Well, Ginger, I guess you must have known Barry before his operation."

The question sounded like a test. How well did I know this girl? How well did she know me? Was she setting an old-fashioned trap to snare a prize like young Barry Munday? It was the female equivalent of Mr. Farley drawing a line between his family and mine.

Without losing the flow of the conversation, Ginger said, "I guess so," and smiled like she knew what the hell was going on.

On the way home in the car, Ginger made me wait. Finally she said, "Do you think maybe you could share this operation with me before I get placed in that situation again, honey?"

The issues raised by the question itself were bad enough, but Ginger Farley calling me "Honey" was madness. I gave myself several minutes of pure silence to formulate an answer. Finally I said, "I went to a matinee one day this summer. One second I was watchin' the previews, and then six hours later I woke up in the hospital. The doctor removed my testicles. Plural; testicles. Both.

"Now you know this is a miracle. You being pregnant is a miracle. I was holed up in my room, feeling sorry for myself, trying to figure out why my life was a waste of time, and then I got the letter from your lawyer. It's like some spiritual barter system. My testicles were taken away, and in return I have a baby in this world. A new direction. A purpose. But don't ask me what happened in the matinee. I don't remember. I have no memory. The doctor said maybe my memory would come back, and maybe it wouldn't. He said my long-term memory could even be affected. I wish I knew what happened."

Ginger didn't say a word. I noticed in the middle of my speech how carefully she was listening. There should be a rule that a man can use the amnesia excuse one time in his entire life. Just once. It should be used at exactly the right moment in a lifetime. It's like a big Mulligan. Use it wisely. I was pleased with myself.

CHAPTER NINE

A FIGURE OF SPEECH

After my sudden increase in productivity at the office, Lonnie Green referred to me with a variety of nicknames. I was "Hoss," "Batman," or "Big Fellow." Of course, Lonnie associated my increase in productivity with his pep talk that morning in the office before I found out about Ginger Farley. Lonnie's pride in me was directly linked to his pride in himself for thrusting me in the direction of success.

Several weeks after the incident with Ginger's parents, Lonnie Green stuck his head in my office door one morning to make an announcement.

"Good morning, Hoss. You busy for lunch today?"

I checked my calendar. "No, all clear."

"Good. Good. An old buddy of mine, Tom Farley, called to see if he could take us to lunch. He specifically asked for you. I'd love to get that piece of business."

I listened with curiosity. "Lonnie, did he say what it was about?"

"No. No, he didn't. How do you know Tom anyway?"

I crafted my answer carefully. "I'm friends with his daughter."

Lonnie made a peculiar corkscrew face. "Oh," he said. And that's all he said. I was left to wade in the juices of doubt and fear.

Tom Farley arrived on time as I knew he would. Lucy buzzed my office to let me know. I walked with Lonnie

Green out to the lobby next to the reception desk. Mr.
Farley's daughter Jennifer stood next to the big man. Her
dress was very short and her smile was big. We stood
together with the common memory of the bathroom fiasco
and my escape through the window. I shook Mr. Farley's
hand and made eye contact on purpose. We all walked out
together to the big black car in the parking lot. I tried to
position myself so Lonnie and I would be in the backseat
together, but Jennifer took a sidestep at the last second and
insisted that Lonnie sit up front with her father. Luckily, I
got the spot in the backseat behind Mr. Farley.

Lonnie Green can keep up a conversation with a tree.
His nonstop chatter limited my involvement. I worked
very hard at keeping my eyes away from Jennifer's legs. I
know her type. They understand the power completely,
and find it funny. There can be no victory with a girl like
Jennifer. Even if a guy finds his way in her pants, it will
never be worth it in the long run. The price is more than
a man can bear.

Jennifer's hand came to rest between us on the
backseat. I glanced at the rearview mirror and caught the
eye of big Tom Farley. In my mind I measured the distance
and angle to determine whether or not the man could see
his daughter's hand on the backseat. It inched closer, the
hand I mean. And then again. She stared out the far
window and like a crab her perfect little hand scuttled up
against my leg. Sudden movements were out of the
question.

I said, "Where we headin' to lunch?"

Lonnie broke into a list of every restaurant within a
ten-mile radius. I just wanted one close by. The hand

slowly scaled the cliff of my thigh and rested momentarily on the bulge of my car keys under the fabric.

I blurted out, "I'm very hungry."

Mr. Farley stared me down in the mirror. If he turned around he would see his daughter's hand. Surely he wouldn't blame me. Surely the man would know the truth.

The index finger of the hand, long and slender, with a candy red nail, extended from the rest of the fingers and touched my zipper. Tap. Tap, tap. And then the finger rested lightly. And finally, with the man still watching me in the mirror, a lovely pressure.

Jennifer snapped her hand away and pointed out the window. "Daddy, there's Angelo's. Can we eat at Angelo's? I haven't been there in forever."

The big car rolled into the restaurant parking lot and came to a stop. I made a necessary adjustment to my Johnson, and we all got out. Mr. Farley and his daughter walked ahead. Lonnie Green seized the opportunity and whispered to me, "Thank God. I thought you were talking about the other daughter." He made that corkscrew face again, and we stepped inside the restaurant.

The conversation centered around Tom Farley's business. Apparently he had a large number of employees, and Lonnie was in high gear to get his hands on this "piece of business," as he called it. I began to wonder if the purpose of this lunch meeting was for Mr. Farley to extend the olive branch and offer himself and his company to me as clients. I refused to look to my right where Jennifer sat. The conversation was very professional.

The restaurant was nearly full. It was a nice place, napkins in laps, glasses of white wine. Across the room I spotted a woman sitting alone with her back to me. My eyes were drawn to her, partially because I couldn't dare look to my right, and partially because of a sense of recognition. The woman stood and turned.

Jesus, it was Lida. And she saw me. There was no hesitation. She was at our table before I could possibly escape. I had a mouthful of food when she said, "So, this is the little bitch."

Lida's eyes cut to Jennifer, who smiled like a cat. I couldn't chew fast enough to interrupt her. I stood. Lonnie and Tom Farley were frozen in their seats. The restaurant became quiet. I could hear myself chew.

I mumbled, "Please, Lida."

Unbelievably, Lida punched me in the stomach with her balled-up broomstick fist. It was swift and furious. I bent over the table, hands to the belly, my internal organs rocked. I lifted my head to see Lida turn to Jennifer and say, "At least he's still got his dick, sweetheart." And she walked out with her head held high.

I swallowed my food and stood for a moment longer, making a supreme effort not to show the pain or the urge to vomit. My mind played the "hole game." I imagined a hole would open up under my chair, and I would fall to the center of the Earth and come out the other side in China, at a big marketplace, full of Chinese people, and vegetables, and chickens hanging from strings. But it didn't happen. It never happens. Instead, I sat down and took a small sip of water. Lida's last statement sat like a spider on the tongues of the people in the restaurant. What could that mean? "At least he's still got his dick, sweetheart."

I looked up at Jennifer and managed to say, "It's just a figure of speech. She's an old girlfriend. Before Ginger. Long time ago."

Lonnie Green said, "Who's Ginger?"

Tom Farley answered, "My other daughter."

Lonnie Green said, "Oh," and made the corkscrew face.

I thought, maybe I could fake like I was having a heart attack. The ambulance would take me from this place, and I could just catch a taxi at the hospital. With my luck they'd probably shock the shit out of me with those heart attack shock things. I'd probably die from the actual shock after my fake heart attack.

Even Lonnie was silent on the ride back. I could feel the backseat shake with Jennifer's uncontrollable laughter. She laughed like her sister, jolly and real.

We pulled up at a stoplight on a four-lane road in the right-hand lane. On the left, next to my window, a van inched up slowly and stopped next to us. The sign read, "Mighty Marvin and the Troll Patrol."

One of the trolls looked down at me from his position in the passenger seat. I saw Tom Farley's head turn and look at the horrible little man. Before the light could change, the troll lifted his fat little hand and clearly flipped me the bird. There was a smile on his face behind the stumpy middle finger. My blood boiled with the memory of the two-hundred-dollar bar tab and the nightmare ride to the hospital in the back of that joy wagon.

Leaning near my face I heard Jennifer ask, "Do you know that man?"

The light changed. The van sped away. Mr. Farley

looked at me in the rearview mirror waiting for an answer. I said, "Of course not."

I think everyone in the car knew I was lying. The swirl of their imaginations probably put the truth to shame. My stomach ached.

CHAPTER TEN

THE EYEPATCH

I drove alone to the office of attorney Newton Creech. In my mind the man would be sharp-dressed, with maybe a small flower pinned to his lapel. There was a sign on the office door with a list of names of lawyers. Newton Creech was in the middle of the list, so I figured he was half in charge.

I stepped in the door and let the receptionist know who I was. "I'm here to sign some papers. I'm Barry Munday."

She giggled. It was a small, reactive giggle, before she had time to stop herself. But it was a giggle.

"Please, have a seat, Mr. Munday. I'll buzz Mr. Creech."

A short, baldheaded man, wearing a golf shirt and penny loafers with a black patch on one eye, came through the door. He looked immediately familiar, but I couldn't place him.

"Mr. Munday, I'm Newton Creech. Good morning."

"Good morning."

He was smiling as he extended his hand. I heard another small giggle from the receptionist. I thought maybe it had nothing to do with me. Maybe she was just a giggler. Then Newton Creech giggled too. It was a brief feminine giggle, but it was enough to abandon my theory of coincidence.

"What's so funny?" I asked.

"Funny?" Newton Creech said. "I don't know. Please

take the time to read these papers, Mr. Munday. The receptionist, Nancy, can notarize your signature."

As the man spoke I tried to look only at his good eye, but I noticed a tiny pinhole in the center of the black patch over the bad eye. I wondered if that bad eye was peeking at me. Maybe it just needed air.

"Have we met before?" I asked.

"I don't think so," he said. "Have you and Ginger picked a name for the baby?"

I hadn't thought of a name.

Mr. Creech said, "Do you know if it's a girl or a boy?"

"No," I said, "Ginger doesn't want to find out. She wants it to be a surprise."

Newton Creech closed his good eye for three seconds. I was sure he tilted his head for the purpose of lining me up in the pinhole of the patch.

"Good luck," he said, and left the room.

After I glanced over the papers I walked up to the counter by the receptionist. She pretended to be looking through a file. I signed my name on several pages and said, "Aren't you supposed to watch me sign this?"

Her body began to shake with silent laughter. I heard a noise behind a door that made me envision four or five people squeezed against the other side. The receptionist turned to me, and I could see she was laughing so hard there were tears in her eyes. I checked my zipper.

"Thank you, Mr. Munday. Have a nice day."

The experience at the law office was like one of those dreams you have when you're half-asleep on the couch on a Saturday afternoon. I drove to the doctor's office to meet Ginger for her appointment. I was early and sat in the parking lot with a pencil and notepad writing baby names. My mind flew across the family tree, movie stars, presidents, and then down the alphabet. The quest seemed important. A name is the first man-made push toward destiny. A name can set in motion a lifetime of grief or happiness.

I met Ginger in the lobby of the doctor's office. We sat in the same place as before, but this time we were alone. Ginger wore the same brown dress. I tried to remember anything else I had ever seen her wear. Nothing came to mind.

I said, "I've been thinking of some names."

"Names for what?" she croaked.

"Names for the baby."

"The baby already has a name."

"What is it?" I asked, and prepared myself.

"If it's a boy, Haywood."

I tried to take a moment to allow the name to settle. To myself, in a whisper, I said, "Haywood. Haywood Munday."

Ginger turned on me and said, "Don't be stupid."

"What do you mean?"

"The baby's last name won't be Munday."

"Why not?" I asked.

"Because we're not married, idiot."

"I don't understand," I said. "I signed all the papers. I stepped up to the plate to be responsible. I love this baby as much as you. It's not your baby, it's our baby. Mine and yours. Both of us. It's not right, and you know it."

We were quiet for several minutes. I heard a baby cry from a back room. I wondered what its name was. Finally

Ginger said, "O.K., you're right. We just won't have a last name. It'll just be Haywood. Lots of famous people through history only had one name."

Again I waited a few moments to let the idea settle.

"Haywood," I said out loud. And then I asked, "What if it's a girl?"

"Cornelia," she answered.

I put my hands up to my face and rubbed my eyes. Nothing was easy with Ginger Farley. I thought, maybe I did have to put something in her drink to get her naked. Otherwise, if she was conscious, I couldn't imagine negotiations between myself and a woman who would want to give her baby just one name. A baby with just one name, Haywood or Cornelia.

I said out loud, "Cornelia," and imagined a tiny baby dressed in pink with a black eyepatch. The nurse opened the door and called us inside.

We went to the same room as before, and I sat in the lone chair against the far wall while a nurse poked and prodded the belly and checked for heartbeats, two separate heartbeats in the same body. The nurse made her exit, and we were left alone again.

I asked, "If the baby is only gonna have one name, why do you get to decide the one name?"

"Why? Because this baby is inside of me, not you. Every minute of every day I'm making a human being. You're not. I have to piss every five minutes. You don't. I have heartburn up in my throat all the time. You don't. I can't sleep right, or shit right, and my breasts feel like two cantaloupes hanging from my chest."

I was surprised at my angry response. "Don't use my

biological disadvantage against me. I'd change places with you in a second. You get to experience a closeness with our child that I can't have. I'll never know what it's like. Never. I go to work alone. I go to sleep alone. You don't. You've got a connection to our baby that I'm not allowed to have."

The doctor entered the room with his usual smile. He said, "How's our baby doin' today?"

We didn't answer.

"Ginger, I need you to step down the hall, give a little blood, and get on the scale."

Ginger left, and the doctor began writing notes in a file.

I asked, "Have you ever had a baby refuse to come out? I mean, have you ever had one grab hold of the sides and just refuse to be born?"

"That's an odd question, Barry. But the answer is no. I've never had one refuse to come out."

"Well, this may be your first."

"Why is that?" he asked.

Suddenly a question popped into my mind that I've always wanted to ask a gynecologist.

"Hey, doctor, can I ask you a strange question?"

"I think you just did."

"No. Another strange question."

"O.K."

"Can you identify your patients by their vaginas? I mean, I've seen a few in my day, and it seems they come in all shapes and sizes. It seems you'd be able to lay out ten vagina photos on the table and place a name to each picture, like witnesses to crimes pick a face out of a photo spread. You think you could do it?"

Doctor Shriver listened closely to my question.

"I suppose I could, Barry. I suppose I could. I'm not sure why I would want to, but I think I could do it."

I imagined, in the doctor's mind, a virtual file cabinet of vaginas. And then Ginger Farley reentered the room. I didn't listen to the conversation between the doctor and Ginger. I began to wonder if it would be possible to re-create the womb in an aquarium. The baby could float in a warm amber fluid in a closed glass aquarium in my living room next to the television. There would be tubes running in and out and a light. I could watch it grow day by day just like it would in the uterus. Every three days I would add a milk-like fluid to the container outside of the aquarium attached to the umbilical cord. At the bottom of the aquarium would be one of those clams that opens and closes, releasing a bubble to the surface. I would watch toes and fingers slowly form. The little private parts would take shape. I could talk to the baby through the glass and explain what a strange world awaits outside the glass walls. I would have to explain that we selected this aquarium method because the natural mother was insane and wanted to just write one name on the birth certificate: Haywood or Cornelia.

CHAPTER ELEVEN

THE BEAVER TREE

For several days after meeting Newton Creech I searched my memory. I was sure I had met the man before, somewhere, somehow, but I couldn't place the face. How could I forget the eyepatch? How many people have I ever met with an eyepatch? It couldn't be many. Or maybe he didn't have the eyepatch when we met. Maybe it was just a lawyer thing, a prop, a sneaky way to get extra attention from the people in a jury.

I got a call from my dumb friend Donald on a Saturday morning. We hadn't spoken since the midget fiasco.

"Barry, it's Donald."

"Hello, Donald," I said.

"Do you remember that night when we were at Redheads?"

"Yes, Donald, I remember. I specifically remember that you disappeared and left me half-drunk in a gay bar being beaten up by three pissed-off midgets. That's what I remember."

Donald hesitated and then said, "I don't know about all that. Anyway, I met a girl that night, Sandy, Sandy Schaffer, tall, stacked. You might have seen her sittin' in the corner that night.

"Let me cut to the chase. We're gettin' married. I'm takin' the plunge again, buddy. Sold the Corvette. She ain't too smart, but I don't much like the smart ones anyhow. Looks like you're all alone out there again."

"Well, congratulations, Donald. You're a lucky man," I said, though I didn't feel it or really care.

"Anyhow," Donald continued, "tonight's the bachelor party. We're gonna go to that new strip joint in the Quarter. I'll pick you up at seven. Just like the old days, Barry, just like the old days."

"I don't think so, Donald. I've got a lot goin' on these days."

"A lot goin' on? What could you have goin' on that's more important than whiskey and naked women? You haven't turned gay on me, have you?"

"No, Donald. I haven't turned gay, though I'm not so sure it wouldn't be a possible option."

"Whatever," Donald said, "I'll be there at seven," and he hung up the phone.

At seven o'clock Donald arrived in a brown Honda. He was happy and stupid as usual, but more so. We found a good parking spot near the river by Jackson Square and sifted our way through the tourists to a strip club on Bourbon Street called the Beaver Tree. I think if I owned a strip joint I could come up with a better name, but then again, "Beaver Tree" says it all. A Lucky Dog vendor was parked outside the club surrounded by the usual group of drunk people holding big cups of hurricanes from Pat O'Briens. People come to New Orleans to do all the things they would never do at home.

Inside the place there were seven or eight round tables surrounded by chairs and a large stage up front. There were naked women on each of the tables smiling and dancing like it was fun. Men sat in chairs around the tables and did things that men always do in strip joints. They drank, shoved dollar bills in garter belts, and gawked like monkeys at a fruit market. I soon joined them.

We met up with two other guys who were supposedly Donald's brothers-in-law-to-be. They were big, muscular young guys from a little town in Mississippi. It was their first strip club experience, and I knew immediately the night would end with trouble. Their names were Toby and Elvis, believe it or not.

Toby stood at the bar looking across the room and said, "Jesus H. Christ, I ain't never seen nothin' like this," and then he threw back a shot of Jack Daniels without a grimace.

The strip joint phenomenon should be the subject of psychological books. Men act like animals in the jungle. They come together from all levels and walks of life to wallow in their common denominator of basic lust. The girls work the room and spot the weak members of the herd to coo and kiss and wiggle money from their fat little wallets. Because we are programed to believe that a woman must like us before we can expect her to remove her clothes, it isn't hard to begin to believe that the gorgeous young girl dancing in the spotlight above has selected us as the only man in the room she actually likes.

Within the first thirty minutes Toby had relinquished his only credit card to the bartender and told the man he had a limit of one thousand dollars. Within the next thirty minutes Elvis said his first words to me, "I think that little blonde likes me." I had seen it all before. I can't count the dollar bills I've pissed away through the years in places like the Beaver Tree starring point-blank into the crab nebulae or placing my face in the void between two massive sweaty breasts.

As I watched Donald put a crisp dollar bill between his teeth and have it removed by the knees of a natural blonde, it occurred to me that Donald was my only friend. It was a sad commentary on a thirty-three-year-old life to admit that my only friend was a man I didn't like. Some people have best friends they keep forever. Friends who keep a person humble through the good times, and afloat during the hard times. A foundation of friends and family that becomes a structure in life to build upon. I've always gone from friend to friend, job to job, distraction to distraction, with the only constant being my devotion to leg. Staring at the naked body in front of me, I wondered if my disgust was due to my physical changes, or my emotional upheaval centered around a baby who waits for me.

At ten o'clock the feature presentation was scheduled to begin on the big stage. We moved our four chairs to the edge of the stage and ordered a new round of drinks. Elvis sat down next to me and said, "The little blonde gave me her phone number."

"Really," I said, knowing from experience that these girls give out wrong phone numbers early in the evening as a way to hook members of the herd and milk them dry by the end of the night.

"What's her name?" I asked.

"Destiny," he said.

"Oh," I said, "that's a very nice name. I hope you two will be happy together."

Elvis looked at me cockeyed and said, "That's a fucked-up thing to say." His attention was soon diverted by a long-legged redheaded woman with a perfect ass.

Coincidences!

A voice came on the loudspeaker, "Gentlemen, our feature presentation for the evening is only a few seconds away. She's tall, she's beautiful, she's built for speed, so let's hear it for the gorgeous, the sexy, Miss Bunny Fu-Fu."

All eyes turned to the spotlight. The curtain opened, and I swear to God, Jennifer Farley stepped out on the stage wearing not much more than a bunny tail and whiskers. My mouth hung open, and I squinted my eyes to be sure it was her.

It had to be her, Jennifer Farley, the daughter of big Tom Farley and the sister of Ginger the toad. Toby slid on his belly across the front of the stage and howled like a hound dog at the moon. Donald pulled him back by his feet before the bouncers had time to come unglued. I just sat there, undulating between my manly desires and the sheer weirdness of it all.

Men threw wadded-up dollar bills, with fives and tens mixed in. I even saw a fifty fly through the air and land silently near Jennifer's high-heeled shoes. She danced. Man, she danced. She was the best I had ever seen. Beautiful and detached like a goddess dancing alone on the beach. She seemed not to notice or care who was watching or who wasn't. My old pal down below stood at attention with no regard for the complexity of the moment.

When the woman was very near the front of the stage, our eyes met. Her face didn't change, but I knew she saw me. Toby reached out his meaty paw and grabbed her on the ankle. I just swung. It was instant. I swung my fist as hard as I could, and it connected against the jaw of Toby. He fell away from the stage on top of the businessman in the next chair.

All hell broke loose. I got hit in the back of the head, and bouncers and bartenders swarmed from every side. When I turned to the stage, Jennifer was gone. I was soon face down on the floor with a large knee planted in my back. From the corner of my eye I could see Toby and Elvis standing back to back in the center of the room kicking and punching in every direction. I half expected Mighty Marvin to appear and save the day. Maybe he'd bring my two hundred dollars.

Right before the cops showed up I heard a voice above me say, "Take him in the back."

I was yanked upright and shoved through the crowd to a room behind the stage. There was blood on the back of my head. I sat in a chair, alone in the room, with a large black man standing half-in and half-out of the doorway. After a few minutes the noise died down. I assumed Toby and Elvis had been taken away to jail, with or without brother-in-law Donald.

The large black man said, "You can leave now."

I didn't ask any questions. I didn't need to. I walked down Bourbon Street with my hand clutched to the back of my head hoping not to see the crazy Mississippi boys. I caught a taxi on Canal Street. First I told the man to take me home, and then, a few blocks later, I asked him to take me to Ginger's apartment. I arrived and knocked at her door around 11:30.

"Who is it?" a voice said through the door.

"Me. Barry."

The door opened with the chain still attached. Without her glasses Ginger looked different. She was wearing a long T-shirt and her belly poked out. She squinted to see me.

"What are you doing here?"

"I just wanted to make sure the baby is O.K."

"Don't be stupid."

"I'm not being stupid." I felt like crying.

"I'm not being stupid," I repeated.

We stood for a moment with the chain still on the door. Ginger said in a soft voice, "The baby's O.K." Then she said, "Go home."

I wondered where that was. I stood outside Ginger's door for almost an hour and then walked home thirty blocks.

CHAPTER TWELVE

FATHER WALSH

I spent a great deal of time thinking about the incident at the Beaver Tree before I came to some solid conclusions. I decided I could use the information about Jennifer to my advantage. By subtle use of blackmail, perhaps I could swing Jennifer to my side and gain a necessary ally in the Farley clan. She could be very useful through the years.

Several days after the incident I received a pleasant call from Mrs. Farley inviting me and my mother to dinner at their home. I accepted the invitation and began to formulate my plan to deal with Jennifer. Surely, I thought, this young co-ed would be afraid of her family learning her secret and therefore willing to go out of her way to help make my life easier.

I picked up my mother at 6:30 and drove to the Farley household.

"Goodness," my mother said, "Why would anyone need a house like this? They must have servants to keep it clean. Is Mr. Farley in the Mafia? Farley isn't an Italian name, is it?"

"No, Mother. Farley isn't Italian."

"Good," she said.

We were met by Mrs. Farley at the door, and my prior dinner adventure seemed to be forgotten. Everyone was correct in their introductions, and my mother seemed to be impressed despite her fear that Ginger had intentions to teach our child to use a sandbox instead of wearing diapers.

I watched Jennifer for the slightest sign of recognition

of our new relationship. She was very good. There was no lingering glance or impure smile. It was obvious I would have to say directly what I needed to say to her. I waited for a moment when we were alone in the kitchen.

"It's nice to see you again, Jennifer," I hinted.

Still with no recognition she said, "Well, Barry, it's nice to see you again also. Do you think you'll be leaving by the front door this evening?"

I politely laughed along with her and retaliated, "Saturday night was pretty wild, wouldn't you say?"

Jennifer looked up at me from the silverware she was sorting and said, "No, not really."

It was only a tiny twitch, just the smallest change in the emphasis on her words, but it was there. Sweet recognition. We understood each other. Maybe she would take a jab at me when we were alone, but I knew I could count on her in front of other people to ease the tension and smooth the rough spots. I smiled, and we headed back to the living room.

There was a knock on the big wooden front door. A priest arrived, and my mother and I were introduced to him. He was apparently the spiritual adviser for the family, and was invited to dinner for some vague religious reason. We all sat down at our assigned seats. On one side of the table Mrs. Farley was flanked by her two daughters. On the other side, I was in the middle with Father Walsh to the left and my mother on the right. Tom Farley sat squarely at the head of the table.

I waited for the touch of Jennifer's toes under the table, but it did not come. My mother remained reserved, but I could tell she teetered on the verge of acceptance. I, on the other hand, felt a new self-assurance with my secret friend, bound by the unspoken threat of revelation. And then the evening took an awful detour.

"Father Walsh?" Jennifer said, "Have you heard the story of young Barry's first dinner with us?"

Innocently, Father Walsh said, "I don't think I have."

She was testing me, I thought. Jennifer was just pushing the boundaries to see the look on my face. Our eyes connected, and she smiled like a mischievous child.

Mrs. Farley piped up, "Jennifer, dear, I don't think this is the time."

"Sure it is, Mother. It's funny. Isn't it funny, Barry?"

I lobbed a veiled threat, "Maybe not as funny as your part-time job."

I expected Jennifer to get the hint and cleverly move the conversation to safer ground. I was wrong.

"Well, it seems our friend Barry has a problem with his aim, if you know what I mean?"

Father Walsh said, "I'm not quite sure I understand."

Surely, I thought, this cannot go on. My mother was listening to the story waiting for some cute little nugget to make her feel warm. Ginger and her father continued to eat like two fat boys at a hotdog buffet. The only person who seemed concerned was Mrs. Farley.

"Please, Jennifer," Mrs. Farley said.

"Well, Father," Jennifer continued, "Barry excused himself from the table and went to the bathroom down the hall. He was gone a long time, and we heard crazy sounds from inside. Water poured from under the door, and Daddy called out to see if Barry was all right."

I said clearly, with a healthy dash of testosterone,

"Jennifer, you've made your point. This is fair warning. If you don't change the subject, you know what's gonna get said. And I don't think you want that to happen."

Jennifer continued to push me. I began to see she simply didn't believe I had the balls to tell her mother and father. It became obvious if I let her run over me in this situation, with both of us knowing the score, I would never, and could never, hold a place of respect in the Farley family, with Jennifer or anyone else.

She just kept going, "Well, it turns out, Father, that young Barry shit all over the floor of the bathroom, took off his pants for some ungodly reason, and then proceeded to climb out the bathroom window and never come back."

I stood from my chair like Caesar rising and called her bluff in a flurry of words.

"Mr. and Mrs. Farley," I said, "Your daughter is not all she pretends to be. Last Saturday night, at ten o'clock, Jennifer was the feature stripper at a nude club in the Quarter called the Beaver Tree."

All eyes were on me. I felt a rush of relief rising to the occasion, drawing my line in the sand, and calling the bluff of that evil little bitch. She underestimated me.

I continued in a slow serious voice, "I'm sorry to be the one to tell you. I know it's embarrassing. It was embarrassing for me to see her like that up on the stage."

Mr. Farley and Ginger remained motionless with full forks half-raised from their plates. Jennifer and her mother had blank expressions, and Father Walsh watched in apparent horror at the news. My mother let slip a sigh of joy at the discovery of a dirty hidden secret about the perfect Farley family in the big house.

Father Walsh was the first to speak.

"Barry," he said, "Last Saturday night, until almost eleven o'clock, Mr. and Mrs. Farley and their daughters were at my house discussing Ginger's pregnancy. We spent the evening together."

I noticed I was still standing. This time there was no bathroom window. My mind flashed back and forth from the Beaver Tree to the people staring at me around the table. Maybe the whiskers threw me off. Maybe the drinks, or the spotlight, or the nakedness. God help me.

After what seemed like infinity, Mr. Farley ended the silence with the words, "Maybe you and your mother should just leave."

I turned to the priest and pleaded, "Are you sure it was Saturday, Saturday night, this last Saturday night?"

He shook his head and said, "Yes, son, I'm sure."

My mother lifted her napkin to her mouth, dabbed daintily on both edges, and said, "Dinner was lovely, but Barry and I really must be going."

Out of a sheer lack of other options, I backtracked.

"I'm sorry. Maybe I'm mistaken. You know, they say everyone has a twin in the world somewhere. Everyone. Haven't you heard that before? I've heard that."

I then added, and immediately regretted, the sentence, "I was a little drunk, and she was dressed like a big rabbit."

It was no use. My mother had the sense to take me by the arm, pick up her purse on the way past the chair, and escort me out to the car.

We drove toward Mother's house in total silence. How could I have been wrong? What happened to my master plan? It was all figured out. In the kitchen Jennifer acknowledged my undeniable advantage. There was recognition.

My mother said quietly, almost to herself, "Why? Why would a man go to a nude club? I don't understand. Explain it to me."

She waited a few minutes for the explanation that would never come and then said, "Have you and Ginger thought of any names for the baby?"

I stared into the oncoming headlights and lied, "No, Mother, not really, but I kinda like 'Cornelia' if it's a girl."

There was silence again, and it began to rain. My mother turned her head toward the passenger window, and I barely heard her say to herself, "Cornelia."

I gave her time to let it settle.

And then she whispered, "Cornelia Munday."

CHAPTER THIRTEEN

PICKLE RELISH AND GO-GO BOOTS

I decided to stay away from the Farley house. Bad things seemed to happen to me there. Ginger and I were getting along fairly well. She appeared to enjoy the fact that I didn't fit neatly with her family. She would often repeat in the middle of our conversations the phrase, "I was a little drunk, and she was dressed like a big rabbit."

The world began to cool a bit in late September. Ginger's sister was home for the weekend. Through pieces of conversations I learned that Jennifer was getting married the first weekend in December, only a few days before the baby was due. I tried not to ask too many questions about Jennifer, or anyone else in the family for that matter.

Ginger called to invite me to a movie with her and Jennifer. I drove to Ginger's apartment to pick them up. When I arrived, Ginger wasn't ready yet. I sat at the far end of the couch away from Jennifer. It was the first time we'd spoken since my plan backfired, and I was asked to leave in the middle of dinner.

Jennifer said, "When you sit still, you're actually a very attractive man."

What did that mean? I decided to just wait and see.

"No, I mean it. Your skin is fresh and lumpy. Touch-able."

I pretended to watch television.

"I'm getting married."

I stared straight ahead and said, "I heard. Who's the

lucky fellow?"

Jennifer answered, "You know him. Newton Creech. Newton Creech, attorney at law." She said the words slowly like she needed to hear them spoken out loud.

"Newton Creech? The guy with the eyepatch?" I blurted out.

Jennifer laughed, "Eyepatch?"

I was confused. "Are we talkin' about the same guy? The guy who sent me the letter about Ginger? Newton Creech, attorney at law?"

"Yes," she said, and then there was a look of understanding.

Jennifer explained, "That was a joke, Barry. He was just playing a joke on you. The eyepatch wasn't real. Don't you know the difference?"

It rang true. The receptionist laughing. The other people behind the door. The tiny pinhole in the eyepatch and the shiny little eye watching me through the hole.

"Why?" I said. "Why would the man wear a fake eyepatch?"

Jennifer laughed at me, "Do you have a sense of humor? Any sense of humor at all? Newton is a funny man. It's one of the things I love about him. He's also hung like a rhino."

I rushed past the visual image and pounced, "Was that really you the night at the Beaver Tree? Was it? Just say. What difference does it make? No one will believe me anyway."

Ginger's bedroom door opened, and she stepped into the living room next to the couch.

Half-interested, she said, "You're not tryin' to steal my

man, are you, Jennifer?"

Both of the girls laughed, and I wondered once again what the hell was going on. Why must every second with these people be uncomfortable?

"You wouldn't happen to have a beer?" I asked.

Ginger was looking for something in the drawer of the end table. She said, "Yeah, I think so. Check the fridge."

The kitchen countertops were lime green. There was a big ceramic cookie jar shaped like Yosemite Sam. The place smelled of fish.

I opened the fridge and stared inside. The entire top shelf was covered with shoes. All colors and styles of women's shoes, and sandals, and one tall pair of white go-go boots. Every other shelf in the entire refrigerator was full of condiments. There were multicolored jellies and jars of mustard. On the door I saw apple butter, sweet pickle relish, martini onions, tartar sauce, bar-b-q sauce, sweet-n-sour sauce, and every other sauce invented since Eve first complained to Adam.

I purposefully didn't turn around to see if the women were watching me, eager for a fresh laugh. I found one beer, hidden on the bottom shelf near the back next to a jar of green mint jelly. The top of the beer can was sticky. I held it to my nose and took a smell. It had the delicate odor of crap. Why would a woman keep her shoes in the refrigerator?

When I turned around, neither woman was paying me any attention. There must be an advantage to keeping shoes cool. What could it be? Did Ginger Farley sit at home at night eating sauces? What chance would my child have in such a place, raised on pickle relish and ranch dressing, pushing aside a boot to get to the honey mustard?

We finally made it to the movie theater. It was the same theater I visited so many months ago when my testicles were taken away. It was my first trip back, and I was itchy and anxious. The night before, I had dreamed that my balls, alone and lost, made their way back to the theater like a dropped-off dog can find its way home from miles away. It was a spooky little dream I tried to forget, but one part kept leaping back in my mind. The little balls, side by side, coming down the aisle of the theater, moving to and fro in a herky-jerky pecking motion. They were the devil's balls, fire red and angry.

The three of us, Jennifer and Ginger in front of me, stood in the popcorn line. Up ahead I spotted the exquisite backside of a well-developed young woman. My eyes progressed up the length of her back, and then she turned her head to the side. I was unable to move. It was the girl I met before. The sixteen-year-old with the traveling hands and violent father. The initiator of my life change. Candice.

I moved to my left to hide behind Ginger. I moved to my right when Candice changed direction, popcorn in hand, heading down the long hall. I crouched and watched from the corner of my eye. The theater had four screens. I hoped to God Candice would be watching a different movie. Ginger and Jennifer didn't seem to notice my odd behavior, and we loaded up with Skittles and Cokes and other overpriced sugar bombs.

Unfortunately, when I turned the corner down the hall, I saw that our particular movie was in the same cinema where my unfortunate incident occurred. I tried to direct the women to a seat in the back, but they seemed to know where they wanted to go. We got closer and closer to the actual row where I sat with Candice, and then Jennifer stopped and sat down in the exact same seat where Candice had sat before. Ginger took the seat on the row and left the middle seat open. The exact same cinema, the exact same row, the exact same seat where I had been so many months before.

I just stood for a moment and pondered the unlikelihood of this coincidence. Of all the theaters in town, of all four cinemas in the theater, of all fifty rows in the cinema, of all twenty-five seats on the row, I was led to the exact location where I was struck so fiercely in the groin by the irate father of a sixteen-year-old vixen who herself was probably somewhere in the darkness. My eyes searched the room in the semidarkness for the face I hoped not to see.

"What's the matter?" Ginger said. "Sit down."

I squeezed past her and sat down. Other people began to come in and sit down around us. It was quiet, and then Jennifer farted loudly. It was a clear and obvious fart. She turned to me and said, "You're disgusting."

Until that moment, I had never heard a woman fart out loud. My married friends had told me about such a thing, but I'd never heard it with my own ears. Mixed with my fears of Candice, and the evil suspicions concerning our seat selection, I was barely able to contemplate the fart itself, much less the accusation. And then she did it again, loud and robust, the fart of a large man upside down on a fraternity house couch.

I said, "What the hell are you doin'?"

"Me?" Jennifer said, and then she leaned over and said loudly to her sister, "Could you ask your boyfriend not to fart? It's embarrassing."

The old couple behind us was quiet, with ears the size of salad bowls. Another woman, sitting alone, made a face of disapproval.

And for the third time, Jennifer farted again. Even louder than the two before. She quickly stood and moved over one seat, leaving an empty chair between us. The sour-faced woman made a point of getting up and moving to the other side of the theater as a statement of her disgust. I started to laugh. I couldn't stop, and I didn't try. Ginger started to laugh, and then Jennifer. It was the first time I felt part of those people. It was the first time we laughed together instead of apart. It felt nice. Ginger patted my leg, and we watched the movie together.

On occasion, during the movie, I turned my head around to search for Candice. She was nowhere. I began to wonder if I had seen her at all. I even began to wonder if I remembered what she looked like. And then I began to wonder how a woman as gorgeous as Jennifer Farley, with a short skirt and heavenly legs, could produce anything like a fart. It occurred to me that possibly everything I've ever known about women was incorrect.

I leaned over to Ginger and whispered, "We're gonna have a baby girl. Don't ask me how I know, I just do."

CHAPTER FOURTEEN

HORNY CORNY

Ginger sat on her couch reading a book.

I asked, "What are you reading?"

Ginger held up the book for me to see. The title was "*The Strangulation of Particus.*"

"Sounds depressing," I said.

Ginger responded, "I hope our child doesn't follow in your footsteps of ignorance. Have you ever read a book in your entire life, besides high school or college assignments, ever, one, just one book?"

She waited for nothing and said, "By the way, my sister invited you to her rehearsal dinner the night before the wedding." She handed me a cream-colored envelope.

I asked, "Isn't that the week before the baby comes?"

"It's the week before the due date, but the baby could come any minute. It feels like it's gonna kick a hole in my side and crawl out right now."

"Can I feel it?" I asked.

Her eyes said, "Yes," and my hand was guided by her hand to the spot. There was a bump, and another bump, and it seemed impossible the little creature on the sonogram could cause such a commotion.

"Does it hurt?" I asked.

"Not really."

"Are you scared?" I asked.

We were still strangers, getting to know each other word by word. For the first time I saw a fear in her face I hadn't taken the time to recognize. There was a tiny person inside of Ginger. A little, hungry, anxious person, waiting to come out. And this little person was bound and determined to come out through a multipurpose hole, which to Ginger Farley, and even to me, seemed virtually impossible. And then there was the umbilical cord, and something they call the afterbirth, and when all the pain of the natural act is done, there is a baby, little, and pink, and loud, who demands to live and suck the engorged breasts, and go to college. At least that's what the baby book says.

Sitting there with my hand on Ginger's belly I thought about the enormous responsibility. Could there be any higher calling in life? Could there be any commitment as serious and long-term as bringing a baby into this world? I don't think so. And in my case, I skirted the edge of impossibility and found a miracle of obligation. I felt the palm of my hand warm with sweat on Ginger's skin, and then another bump, maybe a foot pushing against the walls of its little world. How will it know when the time comes to leave?

"Do you want me to go with you to Jennifer's dinner?"

"If you want," she said.

"No, that's not what I asked. Do you want me to go? Neither one of us can sit here and pretend I'm being invited because they like me. I'm only invited because I'm the father of your baby, and I don't want to be there alone, if you know what I mean?"

"Are you afraid of my family?"

"Yes, I am. Each of them, one by one, separately and together."

Some women detest weakness. They say they want a

sensitive man, a man in touch with his feminine side, but ultimately, they detest weakness. Other women seem to like the knowledge that the weakness exists.

"O.K.," Ginger said, "I would like you to accompany me to my sister's rehearsal dinner."

With my hand still resting on her belly, Ginger lifted her book and began to read again. I had reached new territory in the skirmish between lust and fatherhood. I was struck with the desire to slide my moist hand upward toward the playground of Ginger's growing breasts. My hand pretended to search for baby movement and inched north. Ginger kept reading, and I watched her eyes for the secret signs of approval. My thumb casually grazed the soft fabric underside of Ginger's left breast and moved away gently. I gradually worked my way upward again until my thumb touched home a second time, and I left it there.

Ginger's eyes broke from the words on the page and met my eyes. There was no expression, none, nothing to interpret. In days gone by, this nothingness would have been a green light, the capsulization of everlasting hope. But now, there was indecision, clear, absolute, recognizable indecision, and I removed my hand quickly as I leaned back on the couch next to Ginger. She retreated to reading her book, and we sat there like an old married couple satisfied with the comfort of silence.

I broke the silence with a statement. "I've been thinking about the name 'Cornelia.'"

"Yes," she said, still reading.

"Well, you have to be very careful with names. Other children can be cruel. You have to foresee nicknames."

"Yes," she muttered again, still reading.

"You've got to know that kids will shorten a name. They'll take a name and shorten it down. She'll be called 'Corny.' That's what they'll call her."

There was no response.

I said, "Do you like 'Corny'?"

"Yes. I do."

"Really? You like 'Corny'? You're O.K. with your daughter being called 'Corny'?"

Ginger looked up, "Yes. I am."

I took a deep breath, and Ginger turned the page in her book.

"All right," I said, "And I guess you know what the boys will call her in high school?"

"What's that?" Ginger asked, not looking up.

"'Horny Corny.' That's what the boys'll call her. You can count on it. 'Horny Corny.'"

Ginger looked up and said, "You mean that's what the boys like you will call her. Not everybody, just the boys like you."

She had a point, but I couldn't give up.

"Maybe," I said, "but that'll be her name."

Ginger held my stare and finally said, "I'm not going to mold my life or my child's life around the actions of perverts and degenerates. I'm not going to be afraid of the possible idiocy of people who might call my daughter 'Horny Corny' because it rhymes, or because it's dirty, or because they're too lazy to pronounce her real name, 'Cornelia.'"

She paused and added, "And by the way, the next time you touch my breast without my permission, I'll cut you while you sleep. Do you understand?"

I got off the couch to go to the kitchen. I walked past the spare bedroom of Ginger's apartment, which had slowly become the baby room. Ginger and her mother, with the help of my mother, accumulated baby things. Since nobody but me knew the sex of the child, there was apparently some turmoil over colors for blankets and pillows and other items. I stood in the doorway and looked across the room.

There was a crib. Ginger and I recently had an argument over whether the crib met all the latest safety requirements. Since it came from my family, I was obligated to defend safety features I didn't know existed. The crib was still in the room, so I must have done a good job.

There was a changing table in the corner. On top were lots of little items and bottles. I stood at the table and tried to imagine the purpose of these things. I opened one of the tiny diapers and positioned it on the table like I would if the baby was there with me. It was hard to tell the front from the back. I began to wonder if I would be like parents I see who check a child's diaper by holding the butt-end of the child up to their faces for a whiff, or shove their fingers around the edges to look for poo. I thought, why don't they just have a clear plastic dot on the back of the diaper? When the diaper's dirty, the dot turns brown. You don't have to hold it up to your face or stick your fingers in there. You can spot it across the room and just say, "Look, little Billy took a dump. It's time to change the diaper." Besides, if there was a clear dot on the back you could tell the front side from the back side of the damn thing. But then again, I remembered Ginger said our baby wouldn't wear diapers because of the psychological ramifications.

Next to the table there was a small plastic bottle of gas relief. It seemed odd. What does a baby eat that could possibly give it gas? Tacos? Pinto beans? Don't be stupid. And there were suck toys, and a breast pump, and a gizmo called a "wipe warmer" for warming whatever you use to clean a baby's private parts before changing the diaper. The breast pump specifically caught my attention, and I looked over my shoulder at the doorway before I scanned the drawings of bare breasts in the instruction booklet. Surely I'd be allowed to watch my child feed freely at the breast of her mother.

I wandered to the kitchen and opened the refrigerator. Behind the shoes I found a Coke. The word "titmouse" was written in permanent marker on the aluminum top of the can. Secretly I looked forward to the rehearsal dinner of Jennifer and Newton Creech. Maybe I shouldn't have cared, but I wanted those people to like me. I sat down in a chair across from the couch and opened the cream-colored envelope. Handwritten at the bottom of the formal invitation in blue ink it said, "No farting please."

CHAPTER FIFTEEN

A DRUNKEN PLAN

On the Friday of the rehearsal dinner, almost mid-morning, I got a call from a client. The worst thing about my newfound work ethic was working. The worst part of having clients is having clients. They whine, and bitch, and want their hands held like children. It's part of the job.

Ed Whisenhunt was having his crisis du jour. He wanted to meet me at a bar called "Freddy's" at 5:30 to talk insurance. Lonnie Green decided to come along to make sure I didn't do anything stupid.

I told him, "Lonnie, I've got to be at the rehearsal dinner at seven o'clock, and it's about thirty minutes away from Freddy's."

Lonnie Green said, "I'll drive. We'll have a drink, seal the deal, and break away. I'll get you there on time."

At 5:31 I ordered a bourbon and Coke. Ed Whisenhunt finally arrived at 6:05. I think he did it on purpose. The man knew how badly we wanted and needed his business, and he seemed to believe that part of the price we should pay is waiting. So we waited, and when he showed up we acted like it didn't matter.

Lonnie ordered a round of drinks, and then another. Ed Whisenhunt slowly undressed. With the first drink his jacket came off. With the second his tie loosened. Halfway through the third he rolled up his sleeves and we "got down to business." By then I was borderline drunk, carefully stepping through the minefield of words and phrases in the land of intoxication.

At 7:04 Ed Whisenhunt finally went to the bathroom. His bladder must have been the size of a trash bag.

"Lonnie, I've gotta get the hell outta here. I'm already late."

"We've got him, Barry. Can you feel it? He's ours. Fifteen minutes. That's all we need. Fifteen minutes."

At 7:22 Ed Whisenhunt received a call from his wife and left quickly. I arrived at the club at eight sharp, one hour late. I popped a peppermint and stepped into the bathroom to take a leak and fix my crispy hair. My mother says I have crispy hair.

A large portion of the dining room had been separated for the rehearsal dinner of Tom Farley's daughter. I walked into the room to find a long table with twenty-five or thirty people seated, all eyes immediately on me. There was one empty chair between Ginger and Jennifer at the far end, and I made my walk of shame whispering drunken apologizes before I sat down. I felt the usual burden of unbearable tension in the room as Tom Farley watched my every move from his place at the head of the table.

The waiter asked, "May I get you a drink, sir?"

I whispered awkwardly, "Yes, bourbon and Coke. And make it a good one."

By the time my drink arrived, conversations had sprouted throughout the room, and I grew bold in my anonymity. Scanning the table I saw Newton Creech wearing that idiotic eyepatch one chair away from me on the other side of Jennifer. I didn't know the vast majority of the folks at the table, but there was a black man sitting across from me to the right. He was familiar, and I watched him as I sipped my drink and ordered another.

No one spoke to me, not even Ginger, as I explained to her why I was late and then offered my explanation to Jennifer.

It hit me who the black man was. He was the guy at the Beaver Tree who took me to the back room and stood guard at the door. I was sure it was him, although he wouldn't look back at me, and I had clearly reached the delightful point of intoxication where rationality was slipping away. I smiled and thought, I was right all along. If that's the bouncer from the Beaver Tree, then Jennifer Farley is "Bunny Fu-Fu," and if Jennifer Farley is "Bunny Fu-Fu," then am I the only person in this room who is the butt of the eyepatch joke? Newton Creech must be one hell of a funny man to wear that idiotic eyepatch at his own rehearsal dinner just to make me look stupid. Why hadn't Jennifer told her fiancé that she'd let the cat out of the bag and told me already about the super-hilarious eyepatch gag?

With my next drink, rationality was replaced by a dangerous combination of self-assurance and paranoia. It seemed I was being laughed at. Newton Creech leaned over and winked at me, although truthfully I couldn't tell if it was a wink or just an extended blink.

I said to Ginger, "It would be a shame for Newton Creech, attorney at law, to get his ass kicked the night before his wedding."

A few seconds later Newton Creech leaned forward and said to me, "I see you've been taking those new male lactation pills so you can help breast-feed the baby. Are you supposed to be drinking alcohol?"

I had never heard of such a thing, and for an instant I

was stuck in the quagmire between ignorance and retaliation. I turned to Ginger and asked, "What is he talking about? Do you know what he's talking about?"

Ginger suddenly laughed and spit forward a piece of cheesecake that landed on my empty drink glass. I turned to my left and Jennifer was also laughing. I moved quickly past the quagmire and stood securely on the solid ground of retribution. My drunken mind formulated a drunken plan.

People began to stand and make sappy speeches and toasts about the lovely couple. It was ridiculous, and at the time it almost seemed they were hired actors who had never actually met these demented people. They told college stories and childhood secrets, all videotaped by a hired cameraman with his tripod set up in the corner. I waited. I waited patiently. How much should a man endure before he fights back? The time had come.

I stood, glass of wine in hand, raised in a toast. There was silence. The odor of the unknown. I heard a female voice at the far end of the table whisper, "Who is that guy?"

I began, "They say a man can be judged by his friends."

I set the glass of wine down on the table and moved to my left past Jennifer Farley directly behind Newton Creech. He kept his head forward and did not turn to watch me. The video camera rolled.

I continued, "Then I would tell my friend Newton Creech, look around this table. Take a look at all your friends."

My hands were resting on Newton's shoulders. I

remember smiling as I said, "Take a long, good look." And in a swift instant my right hand reached around to the man's face and pulled off the black eyepatch. With confidence I thought to myself, I will be the fool no more. I stood behind Newton Creech, eyepatch dangling in my hand, and looked directly across the table at a bridesmaid whose face was locked in horror.

I remember thinking, perhaps she was also the butt of the eyepatch scam? Perhaps her face only shows the horror of my swift action? But there was silence. No laughter. Shock. I leaned down over Newton's shoulder, slowly, to see. And there it was. A glassy white eye. Puffy and dead. Milky rotten.

I stood alone in the room prepared to die. I had yanked off the eyepatch of Newton Creech at his rehearsal dinner, in front of his friends and family, on videotape, the night before his wedding, and now I stood drunk with the black eyepatch in my hand, and then Tom Farley rose. His mouth opened to speak and to my right Ginger said softly, "Oh my God, my water just broke."

My eyes went to the glass of water next to her plate. Jennifer stood and took control like a field general. I was too confused to thank God for the distraction. People were in a frenzy, and we rushed out of the place to go to the hospital like a fire drill. There was no room in Mr. Farley's car. I was in no condition to drive, and besides, my car was across town at my office. The large black man volunteered to take me to the hospital.

As we were riding along I realized the eyepatch was still in my hand.

I said, "Can you give this to Newton when you see

him? It's his eyepatch."

"Oh, I know what it is. I just watched you yank it off his head. That was the craziest shit I ever seen."

It was dark, and I couldn't really get a good look at the man without staring.

I asked, "Have we met before?"

There was a speck of hesitation. "I don't think so."

And then the man said, "Is this your first baby?"

"Yes. My first, and only."

"I've got three, two girls and a boy. There ain't nothin' like it in the world. I don't care how tough you think you are, when that baby comes out into this world, your baby, you're gonna cry, and you won't even try to hide it. And when you pick that baby up in your arms the first time, everything's gonna change. Everything."

And then we came to an intersection. The light was red. We stopped. Across the street, stopped at the light in the opposite direction, stood the van of Mighty Marvin. I could see Marvin behind the wheel with the hanging lightbulb swinging in the background.

I pointed and said, "That son-of-a-bitch owes me money."

The black man focused across the street, obviously reading the words on the side of the van illuminated in the streetlight.

"The midgets owe you money?"

"Yes," I yelled. "Follow 'em. Follow the bastards."

The light changed to green, but we didn't move. The van pulled forward, and I swung my head around to watch it go.

"What's the matter?" I yelled.

In a very calm voice the black man said, "Your girlfriend is having your baby. Maybe right now. What's more important, the birth of your first child or a van full of midgets who owe you money?"

I turned halfway around until we were face to face. He was right, of course, but it didn't soothe me immediately. We were silent as we rode along and arrived at the hospital. He turned into the parking lot to drop me off. I was still wearing the shirt and tie I'd worn all day. I smelled bad.

"You smell bad," the black man said.

"I know."

"Hey, don't be afraid. Watch everything. Take pictures. Tomorrow you'll be somebody's father."

I made my way through the maze of corridors and hallways in the hospital until I stumbled into the lobby of the baby ward. Newton Creech sat alone in the lobby.

"Where is everybody?" I asked.

"They're in the back with Ginger. Where's my eyepatch?"

"I gave it to the black guy."

He squinted his face, and I got another look at the rotten eye.

"What black guy?" he asked.

"The black guy who was at dinner. He drove me here."

Newton held up his hands in disbelief. "I don't know that guy. He was the date of one of the bridesmaids. I never met that guy in my life until tonight."

I ran out of things to say.

Newton spoke out of turn. "You gave my eyepatch to

the black guy who drove you here?"

I thought of something to say. "Yes, Newton, I did. I'm sorry. I'm sorry for everything, but by this time tomorrow I'll be somebody's father, and we'll get you a new eyepatch. I promise."

It seemed to be enough. He sat down, and I went through the double doors. There were nurses back and forth. I was led to the delivery room where Ginger was resting in a hospital bed. Mr. and Mrs. Farley and Jennifer were in the room. Ginger had an IV in her arm and gizmos hooked up to her belly. It was a nice room. There were a few comfortable chairs and a television.

"Is everything O.K.?" I asked.

Ginger answered, "Everything's fine. The contractions are far apart, and I'm only four or five centimeters dilated, so it could be a long time." The word "dilated" made me nervous.

She was calm. It was good to see her calm. Somebody needed to be.

Ginger had a plan. She said, "Barry, why don't you go home and take a shower, change clothes. Jennifer will drive you home on her way to my apartment to pick up my bag and let the cat out."

"You have a cat?" I asked.

Mr. Farley said, "Are you a complete moron?"

Ginger intervened. "Daddy. Please."

I didn't know she had a cat. I never saw a cat over there. Never mind.

Jennifer and I met up with Newton Creech and went to Mr. Farley's car. I got in the backseat. Newton talked to Jennifer as if I wasn't there.

"Guess where my eyepatch is?"

"Where?"

"Barry gave it to Lori's date."

"Joey?"

"I don't even know his name."

"Why?" Jennifer asked.

"Why? How can you ask a man why he would give away my eyepatch when he's the same man who pulled it off my face at our wedding rehearsal dinner in the first place? There's no why."

I thought about explaining Jennifer's confession to me that the eyepatch was a practical joke, but it didn't seem worth the trouble. I thought about revealing my knowledge to Newton Creech that good old "Joey" was the bouncer at the Beaver Tree where his wife-to-be, "Bunny Fu-Fu," did the naked dance in the heart of New Orleans. Instead, I took a private moment to imagine Newton and Jennifer entangled in ecstasy, face to face, with the lights on, and Jennifer turning any which way possible to avoid staring into the milky white eyehole. It was a wonderful thing to imagine, and I actually laughed out loud.

CHAPTER SIXTEEN

PLUM SHRAPNEL

I stood in the shower a long time. The cleansing was more than just physical. My headache pounded under the stream of water as I slowly turned the knob to make it colder and colder until my breath caught sharp from the chill. I took four aspirin, brushed my teeth, and proceeded through the preemptive program to stop a hangover in its tracks. I stood in the bedroom wearing my best pair of underwear. What does a man wear to his baby's birth? First impressions are enormously important. When the baby comes out, and sees me for the first time, the image will be embedded in the memory of my only child forever.

People say, "Babies don't remember anything about the day they're born." I say, "We remember a lot more than we remember." I selected my best shirt and tie, a new pair of pants, clean socks, and dress shoes.

I called a taxi to drive me to my car at the office. On the way out the door I had an idea. We really only have one birthday, the day we are born. All the rest of our birthdays are only anniversaries of the original. A person should have a birthday cake on their only birthday.

By the time I drove to the all-night grocery store it was after 1:00 A.M. I selected a long white sheet cake with red icing and flowers around the edges. The only person behind the cake counter at the back of the store was a janitor mopping the floor.

"Is there anyone here who can write 'Happy Birthday' on a cake?"

The old man smiled the smile of a man looking for a diversion, any diversion at all.

"I can hep ya."

He searched and found the icing tube, lined up the cake on the counter, and said, "What do it need to say?"

"Happy Birthday, Baby."

The old man smiled again, and I could see his bottom lip full of black tobacco. His teeth were dark yellow, the color of old ivory figurines, carved in his head. It wasn't until he finished his chore that I learned the old man couldn't spell. He went back to mopping, and I stood in the grocery store at the cake counter looking at my cake. "Happy Birthday, Babby."

On the way from the back of the store to the checkout line I passed through the baby food aisle. It dawned on me, no one remembered to buy baby food. What will the child eat when we leave the hospital? I was proud of myself. No one else seemed to remember this important detail.

It was a flea market of flavors. I picked out "butternut squash & limas," "plum/banana explosion," and "meatloaf and mashed potatoes." I was mesmerized by the selection. There were colors and combinations, big jars and little, vegetables, meats, and fruits. I knelt down with the cake box on the floor selecting baby food. The store was very quiet. I felt a sensation, unexplainable. I looked up from my spot on the floor. Lida Griggs stood, arms crossed, with that God-awful dog, watching me, at the very far end of the aisle.

There was a moment of panic, a clear vision of the future, the realization that nothing good could come from this encounter. I stood, cake box in hand, jars of baby food resting on the top of the box. And then I ran. I heard the bark of the beast behind me as I flew past the cake counter and through the double doors into the back of the store. The old janitor sat on the top of an upside-down bucket, mop in hand.

"Help me," I begged. "There's a dog. A huge dog."

The double doors burst open behind me, and I ran forward without turning. There were boxes and crates stacked against the walls. A baby-food jar slid off the cellophane cake box and exploded at my feet, spraying plum shrapnel all over my favorite khaki pants. The giant dog lumbered after me around each corner and down the hall. As I ran I shoved jars of baby food in my pocket. Up the stairs, through a door, down the stairs. I stopped and turned. No dog. No Lida. Quiet. I stood still and listened. Nothing.

A drop of sweat rolled peacefully down my forehead and got lost in the eyebrow. I tiptoed slowly toward the light coming from the window of a set of double doors down a side hall. I eased open the door with my shoulder and peeked out into the bright supermarket. There were two young guys arguing in front of the beer display. I slowly crept forward, eyes searching for the movement of the beast, and proceeded down the aisle near the two guys. They stopped arguing and watched me.

Before I could speak a word, the double doors thirty yards behind me crashed open. I turned, still holding my baby's birthday cake, and watched Lida's Great Dane galloping like a hound from hell across the white linoleum. In one fluid movement I grasped the cake with one arm and with my free right hand pulled from my pocket the jar of "butternut squash," raised my arm, and with great velocity threw a baby-food bullet directly between the eyes of the giant dog.

The effect was instantaneous. The animal stopped, stiffened, and fell over in a heap like the carcass of a deer. The two beer guys watched it all. One of them whispered, "Wow."

I turned and ran, digging out my wallet, balancing the cake, and throwing a wadded up twenty-dollar bill toward the fat lady at the register before I passed through the front door. The coast was clear. No Lida. I reached my car, tossed the cake in the passenger seat, and sped away toward the birth of my child, digging jars of baby food from my pants pocket, and praying silently for God to spare the life of the beast.

CHAPTER SEVENTEEN

THE TOURIST

My mother was in the lobby of the baby ward along with Jennifer, Newton, Mr. and Mrs. Farley, and several other people I recognized from the rehearsal dinner. A nurse led me to a room where Ginger and the baby would stay after the delivery. I dropped off the cake and baby food before being led briskly to the delivery room.

Ginger rested comfortably upright watching the television across the room.

"Is everything O.K.?" I asked.

"Yes. I'm going to have the epidural in a few minutes. The contractions..."

She stopped midsentence with pain in her face. I stood next to the bed and held her hand. A different doctor came and asked me to step out while he "administered the epidural." He described a gigantic needle, and I left the room immediately. Waiting by the door I expected screams, but there were none. After ten minutes the doctor left, and I went back inside to stand awkwardly in my place.

I felt like a tourist, camera in hand, standing in the middle of a foreign circus. Everyone else seemed to have a place. The nurses knew their roles. Ginger and the baby were essential to the plan. Even the people in the lobby waited patiently in a place they clearly belonged. Who was I? Where did I belong? Should I sit down and watch TV.? Or maybe get more involved in the medical procedures and instruments? I snapped photographs of

Ginger, and the nurses, and tried to be funny. I learned quickly that nothing was funny, especially for Ginger. Even the funny stuff wasn't funny.

Ginger's parents and sister came in and out of the delivery room. They were nervous and excited and we shared at least a temporary bond of common anxiety held together by tiny spider webs of civilized glances and comments.

"Are you nervous, Barry?" Tom Farley asked.

"Yes, sir."

"In the old days the men just stood out in the lobby smoking cigars and waited."

"I'm not so sure that's a bad idea," I said.

At 6:05 A.M. Ginger was eight centimeters dilated and the contractions were intense. Of course, with the epidural, Ginger lay quietly with her dead legs and watched the monitor. Balls of sweat appeared on her forehead, and I wiped them off with a rag.

Ginger said, "What's on your pants?"

Plum stains spotted the front of my trousers, with the biggest stain directly on my penis area. I looked down and tried to remember if they were the same pants I abandoned in the Farley bathroom long ago. Surely not?

I lied, "Well I don't know."

"You're lying," she observed. "You smell like fruit."

"O.K., I'm lying, but if I told you the truth it would take too long, and you're gonna have a baby, and it doesn't matter anyway."

"Where's your helmet?" she asked.

"What?"

"Remember, the doctor said that any man who faints

at the sonogram is sure to pass out during delivery. We think it would be best for you to wear a helmet so if you fall over nobody will have to stop and take care of you."

I remarked, "Oh, I see, it's only me that can't be funny."

She was too nervous to be mean. We smiled together, and the delivery doctor came into the room for the first time.

"O.K., guys, here we go. Let's see where we are."

Legs were lifted to stirrups. I stayed by the head. The doctor poked and prodded down there.

"Here we go, guys. You're gonna have a baby."

It was 7:15 A.M. A rerun of "The Waltons" was on the television across the room. It was the episode where Mary Ellen decides she wants to be a doctor, and she refuses to let anyone stand in her way. I considered it to be a good omen.

The door to the delivery room was closed. The doctor rolled to his position between the legs of Ginger on a small black stool. The nurse positioned instruments on a table nearby, and Ginger began to push. Her face showed pure fear. I stood next to the bed. My gut instinct told me to leave the room. Go away. This is woman business. It's like watching an eclipse. It just shouldn't be done. But as Ginger pushed, and the doctor did his work, curiosity pulled me forward until my head leaned over directly above Ginger's private parts. Lust had no place in this new world. That mysterious crevice had a higher purpose than my lost soul could fathom.

"Do you see the head?" Dr. Shriver asked.

I could see something gray and shiny. If I hadn't

known where I was, if I was from a distant planet, and I was asked to guess what was coming from that hole, one of my last guesses would be a baby. I reached down and touched the head with my finger. Ginger pushed again, and then again, and the shiny gray surface grew a tiny bit larger with each push, until a face popped out, alien and gray with a tint of yellow, and looked up at me. And then there was a baby.

"It's a girl."

I took a picture. And then another. A white cord hung from the baby's belly, and the doctor snipped and patched and then held the baby up for a photo with the wall clock and the television in the background. Later I could see Mary Ellen Walton holding out her hands in disbelief that her mother and father would discourage a woman from being the very best she could be.

When that baby came out into this world, I remember my clear thought, unrehearsed and unanticipated. I actually said out loud, "Good luck." Good luck, little baby, in this crazy-ass world. Good luck in this life, with all the wonderful mysteries and horrific fears. You can be the smartest baby ever born, and work harder than even Mary Ellen Walton, but you still need luck. Blind, old-fashioned, flip-a-coin, right place at the right time luck.

Men who have experienced watching the birth of their children had all given me the same advice. "Follow the baby." The things that happen afterwards aren't to be seen.

A nurse came in the room and took the child to a corner and began putting drops in her eyes and other things. I talked with Ginger and kept my head away from the activities going on at the business end of the room. I accidentally got a glimpse of needle and thread. There was a blue bowl that contained something that looked like liver. "Follow the baby," I repeated. "You can never go wrong."

A nurse cleaned and wrapped the child. Ginger held our daughter in a ball of blankets. The black man was right. I began to cry. In fact, I'd been crying all along and hadn't even noticed. The nurse handed me the baby, and we headed toward the nursery. There are times in a man's life of great joy or great misery that cannot be compared. It was a crystal moment, a time to see myself clearly.

I walked my daughter down the hall through a locked door into the bright nursery. Window shades were raised, and I held the baby next to the glass for everyone to see. Tom Farley and his wife stood next to my mother and Jennifer and the others. I tried not to look at the still-naked eye of Newton Creech and suppressed the fear rising in my mind of the child seeing such a sight and needing therapy twenty years later because she is unable to remove the image. My mother reached her tired old hand to the glass and touched.

I left the baby with the trusted nurses and went back to Ginger. She was asleep, and I sat with her for at least an hour as the nurses silently came and went. I left Ginger and walked back to the nursery window. The lobby was empty. Everyone had gone home to clean up and regroup. I stood at the big window and stared at my baby alone under the lights. I never really looked at a baby before, little, wrinkled, and slightly yellow.

A strange man wandered up to the window next to me. We stood for a moment, side by side, looking at my baby.

The man said, "We don't see many Chinese babies around here."

"What?" I said, as I looked at the man and then back at the baby girl.

The strange man said, "That baby there's Oriental. Ain't no doubt about it." And then he turned and wandered away to the elevator.

I stood alone at the window and processed this information. I looked across the nursery at the other babies, white and black, to compare. My baby did look different, but then again, so did Ginger. I wondered if maybe one of us had a recessive Asian gene that could explain the soft black hair and the different eyes. God, she was beautiful. So tiny and new. A window from herself through me and back out again into this world. And she was mine, a part of me, a miracle directly from God. All I could see when I looked through the glass was the most beautiful baby ever born.

really!?

CHAPTER EIGHTEEN

CORNELIA AND THE FINE DETAILS OF
BREAST-FEEDING

Around two o'clock in the afternoon they moved us to a regular room down the hall. The baby was rolled in on a table wrapped tight with a pink little hat. I sat in the chair next to Ginger's bed and listened to the husky nurse.

"My name is Norma. We haven't met yet. I'll be here with you, in and out, until the end of the shift this evening. The baby is just fine. She's all clean and hungry."

I stood up and walked across the room to retrieve the jars of baby food. On the way I announced, "I thought about that last night and stopped at the store. I've got 'meatloaf and mashed potatoes' and 'yellow pudding.' Which one do you think would be best?"

Nurse Norma watched me with heavy eyes. She turned to Ginger and then back to me.

"Sir, newborn babies require breast milk."

"O.K.," I said. "She can have it later. Can she have any cake?"

I began to realize Nurse Norma was on the fast track to the conclusion that I was a complete idiot. No one bothered to tell me that babies can't eat baby food, or birthday cake, or pork chops for that matter.

Ginger broke the brief silence. "What's the cake for?"

"It's her birthday. Her only birthday she'll really ever have. It's the day she was born, and I thought a birthday cake would be appropriate."

Nurse Norma walked over to where I stood and

looked down at the cake through the cellophane.

"Who's 'Babby'?"

"Babby?" Ginger repeated.

I acted like I hadn't noticed before and played angry that the person at the grocery store would make such a mistake.

"That's ridiculous. I oughtta take the damn thing back."

Nurse Norma shuffled away from me and asked, "Do we have a name for the baby yet?"

"Cornelia," Ginger answered with a proud smile.

Nurse Norma lifted the baby and placed her in her mother's arms.

"Will the father be joining us?" Norma asked innocently.

It seemed like an odd question. Who the hell did she think I was? My eyes caught with Ginger's eyes and there was no hesitation, "Barry's the father. He was with me through the birth. He did better than I did."

Nurse Norma was embarrassed. She was one of those large women who turn pink in the face and neck as a side effect of the tingle of public embarrassment. Splotches began to form and slowly grew to birthmark-size stains.

"I'm sorry," she whispered, and resorted to her speciality, the fine details of breast-feeding.

I must admit, I was looking forward to the breast-feeding thing. I once saw a woman at the Laundromat breast-feeding her baby in full view sitting in a chair by the Coke machine. I pretended not to notice and walked past the woman several times, stealing peeks at the creamy white breast top and hazel nipple.

Nurse Norma pointed out a videotape we could watch later for breast-feeding demonstrations and instructions. She proceeded to explain positions to hold the baby, nipple tenderness, and frequency of feeding. I listened and nodded my head when needed.

"Now, Ginger, your milk won't come in for at least four or five days. In the meantime, the baby will get a clear substance called colostrum. It is very important to the baby's growth."

I blurted out, "What does it taste like?"

The two women looked at me, and I decided perhaps I had reached a place in the proceedings where silence was my friend.

"Sometimes you'll have to move the baby around to different angles to help her latch on properly. And also, you'll notice sometimes she'll stop sucking and just hang around the restaurant with momma. It's O.K. She'll get what she needs. Are you ready?"

I leaned back in the chair to disappear slightly. It seemed I would be allowed to stay and watch the glorious event. Norma took the baby back from Ginger and asked Ginger to position herself and her breast for the feeding. Ginger rolled her eyes in my direction, obviously trying to hide her discomfort from Norma. I just raised my eyebrows and fought back an improper smile.

The breast was unveiled, plump and magnificent. Much better than I had imagined, with the possible exception of a very dark nipple, which I later learned is a product of pregnancy. Ginger placed her left hand under the right breast and directed the pointy nipple into the waiting mouth of the baby. The child began to suck without explanation, and Ginger let out a grunt.

"Oh my God," she said.

"What's the matter?" I asked.

Norma explained, "The sucking on the nipple by the baby causes the uterus to contract and begin shrinking back to regular size. You'll feel these contractions for several days. They're normal."

Norma left and I watched the baby against her mother's breast. It was the last time lust and breast-feeding had an association. I learned quickly that the female breast, just like that other female part, actually exists for a purpose far beyond my personal sexual and psychological satisfaction. In fact, this knowledge, and the effect of this knowledge, would linger. The boob lost its magic for a spell. It's like the difference between a lamp with a genie, and just a plain old lamp. They may look the same from the outside, but God knows, without the genie, what's the point?

Throughout the day friends and relatives flowed in and out of our room with flowers and presents and stories about the day their own children were born. Maybe the cake was a stupid idea, but every woman who heard the story said the same thing. "That's sweet. How cute." I ate the third "b" in "Babby" to spare us from answering the same question over and over again.

Nurse Norma would take the baby for several hours at a time back to the nursery. Ginger and I were both exhausted, but there would be plenty of time to sleep later, I thought. On one occasion, when the two of us were left alone, I asked politely, "So...are you still leaning toward the name 'Cornelia'?"

"Yes."

"Is there room for discussion?"

"No."

"Have you already filled out the birth certificate?"

"Yes."

"Is there a last name?"

"No."

"You have to give the baby a last name."

"No, you don't. Did Jesus have a last name? Or Moses? Or Calvin?"

"Who's Calvin?" I asked.

Nurse Norma came back through the door rolling the baby to us again. Newton and Jennifer were getting married somewhere across town, and the flow of relatives had slowed to a pleasant crawl. I listened to Nurse Norma talk nurse-talk before she turned to me and said, "Would you like to change her diaper?"

It was a challenge. "Yes, I would."

Cornelia was unwrapped in front of me, leaving a tiny, clean, naked baby screaming with a pitch and frequency unknown to me previously. I understand the correlation of the sucking reflex to the instinct to survive. I understand the baby sleeping, or cuddling against her protector, but I have no understanding of the purpose of a full-throttle scream. If we had been living in the woods, or a cave, I would be forced to fight off the hungry wolves drawn to the piercing cry of a vulnerable infant.

"How do I make it stop?"

Nurse Norma responded calmly, "It's a she, and she won't stop until you change the diaper, and we wrap her up warm again."

I fumbled with the Velcro tab. Norma pulled it for me, and the woman remained unnaturally calm. I pulled the other tab and folded the diaper back.

"What the hell is that?"

The diaper contained a black tar substance that had the look of pure and noxious odor, yet there was no smell. I wiped and rubbed while the baby screamed and the wolves circled. When I was finished, Norma wrapped Cornelia tight in blankets, covered her little head with the little hat, and held her tight against her bosom. Cornelia stopped crying, and I was glad.

After the wedding we received more guests, but finally it was quiet. There was a large green chair in the corner that appeared to have the ability to fold down into a small uncomfortable bed. Ginger and I hadn't discussed my spending the night. When she fell asleep I unfolded the green bed, found a blanket in a drawer, and lay down in my clothes. I turned down the volume on the television as far as it would go and pressed the remote control to begin the breast-feeding video.

I eased the volume upward in hopes I could hear something interesting. When I turned my head, Ginger's mother was standing at the door watching me sitting alone in her daughter's hospital room staring at a breast-feeding video.

I lied, "Did Ginger fall asleep? She was watching this video and I guess she finally dozed off."

I fumbled with the remote control trying to stop the videotape and then trying to locate a sporting event on a regular channel. Mrs. Farley touched Ginger's head and said, "Good night." A few minutes later I turned off the television and fell asleep thinking about the rising cost of college, boys with bad intentions, Ginger's mother catching me watching unfamiliar breasts, and holding my baby's hand when she takes her first step.

CHAPTER NINETEEN

A FOREIGN HAND

During the first night in the hospital I learned my place on the priority list: last. Nurses came in the room every few hours with the baby for feeding, or with medicine for Ginger, and they didn't give a damn about the man sleeping on the brick-hard green multipurpose chair folded into a bed. I was in and out of sleep all night long until I had a dream someone crawled under the covers with me and pressed their body against mine like a spoon lined up from behind. In my dream it was big Nurse Norma, and then the face changed to Ginger, and then a cool hand slid down the top of my pants.

At a critical point I had the sudden realization that my dream was no dream at all. Someone was actually under the covers with me, curved and folded against my backside, with a hand completely down the front of my pants. There are few sensations capable of matching the touch of a foreign hand in a man's pants.

I opened my eyes and across the room could see Ginger asleep in her hospital bed with her face toward the far wall. Before I could crane my neck backwards, Jennifer's voice said, "Good morning, baby."

Without moving I whispered, "What are you doing here?"

"You didn't think I'd actually marry that goofball, did you?"

Jennifer's long fingers encircled and squeezed my forgotten friend.

"Ginger's gonna wake up. Have you lost your freakin' mind?"

Jennifer put her wet lips against my ear and said, "It's always been you. Always. Even before you met Ginger. Give it to me. Gimme the love stick, Popeye."

There was a soft knock on the door, and I believe my heart came to a dead stop. Jennifer leapt from her place on the green bed to a standing position, peering out the open window glowing with the first light of morning.

Mr. and Mrs. Farley quietly crept into the room along with Newton Creech. They gathered around Ginger's bed as she awoke. I was afraid to close my eyes and therefore simply lay in a prone position, eyes wide open, waiting for someone to speak. Anyone. Any words.

Jennifer, somewhere behind me, apparently pushed Play on the VCR under the television.

"Barry, you little rascal, did you enjoy the breast-feeding video?"

Mrs. Farley looked up and then away quickly, embarrassed for me but unwilling to defend. Nurse Norma came through the door pushing the baby on the little table, all wrapped up again like a doll. Jennifer skipped to Newton's side, arms sliding neatly around his waist, and said to Ginger, "We postponed our honeymoon for one day to make sure you and Cornelia are O.K."

I rose from the stone bed and put on my shoes. We all exchanged "good mornings" and I announced my intention to go downstairs to the cafeteria. A peek in the bathroom mirror revealed my hair in all directions and the need for a shave. The touch of Jennifer's cool hand down below hung around in my mind, and I knew it would remain a place to visit for years to come.

I walked past the empty nurses' station and through the double doors into the lobby area. The shades were up on the nursery windows. A man stood alone with his hands behind his back watching the babies. Normally I would have passed him by without a thought. But today, this Asian man, mid-twenties, black hair, swallowed my attention. I slowed my pace and tried to see if he was watching any particular baby. Past him, down the hall a bit, standing at the elevators, I kept my eye on the Asian man, maybe Chinese, or Japanese, how can you tell? He never looked in my direction, the elevator arrived, and I stepped inside.

I hurried through the cafeteria line, coffee, sausage biscuit, so I could get back to the lobby. When I arrived the man was gone, and my mother sat in a chair against the far wall alone. I sat down beside her.

"Well, son, did you get any sleep last night?"

"No."

"Get used to it," she smirked.

"Mom?"

"Yes."

"I need to ask you a question about my father. I know we never talk about him. I know the rule, but I need to find out something."

My mother pretended to dig through her big blue purse.

"Just tell me this, Mom, just tell me where he came from. What country?"

I took a bite of my delicious sausage biscuit while my mother pondered my request. I expected nothing, but hoped for an answer. My deliberate inattention was a ploy to disguise my need and maybe lull my old mom into letting a few secrets slip through the cracks. The silence lasted almost longer than I could stand.

"Your father came from a faraway place, and he should have stayed there. He left behind the only part of himself worth knowing: you."

Her answer left no room to maneuver.

"Mom, I don't know much about babies. Does my baby look O.K. to you?"

"Don't be a fool, Barry. Do you think it was just a coincidence that you lost your testicles in that theater accident, and then, out of the blue, shazam, you learn about this little baby? Well, of course not. God has His ways. Don't turn your back on Him, and don't let the devil crawl back in your head and twist you all upside down again."

I took another big bite of my biscuit. It was truly delicious. The sausage was tender and spicy. The biscuit was golden brown and hot inside. I wanted it to last forever.

"Mom, almost everyone who has come to see us at the hospital since the baby was born are friends or relatives of the Farleys. Why don't I have any friends?"

"You've been busy."

We left it there, and I sat for a while. I started to offer my mother a bite of the sausage biscuit but decided not to run the risk that she may accept the invitation. I was sad to place the last bite in my mouth and wash it down with a swallow of warm coffee.

The Farleys were leaving when my mother and I

entered the room. Everyone was cordial, but I was glad to see them leave, especially Jennifer, with those long and powerful fingers.

I held the baby in my arms. She seemed to be trying with all her might to open her eyes and see the world. It was like she was trapped inside this tiny helpless body with no way out except to open her peepholes to the outside. I remained baffled by her crying. What could she be so pissed off about? Tell me, please.

My mother held the baby and walked in half-circles around Ginger's bed. She talked in a nauseating repetitious baby babble, constantly asking the child questions.

"Is her hungry? Is her all warm? Is her happy?"

From nowhere, still looking at the baby, my mother asked, "Have you decided on a name?"

Ginger, as usual, seized the opportunity to defend.

"Yes. Cornelia."

My mother answered quicky, "Cornelia? That's nice."

There was a fat silence.

"Cornelia what?" my mother asked, still looking at the baby.

Sometimes it's best just to let a train run its course. I listened.

"Just Cornelia," Ginger explained.

My mother said, "No middle name?"

Ginger countered, "No middle name, and no last name."

My mother repeated, "No last name?"

"No ma'am," Ginger said respectfully.

"But you've got to have a last name."

Ginger explained, "Jesus didn't have a last name, or Moses."

I waited a moment and said, "Or Calvin."

"Who's Calvin?" my mother asked.

I answered, "I'm not quite sure, Mother, but he must have been a very important man. And he only needed one name."

The three of us looked at each other a few times like strangers. My mother went back to asking the baby ridiculous questions, and the subject was never raised again. Long live Calvin, whoever the hell he is.

CHAPTER TWENTY

MOE

I noticed young Cornelia was unable to hold up her head. I didn't want to blurt it out and cause alarm so I asked Nurse Norma to step out in the hallway.

"Nurse, I know you know what you're doing, but I think maybe the baby has a problem with her neck. She can't hold her head up, it just bobs around like it's not connected right. No offense, but I'd like you to call Dr. Shriver to come take a look. Today's Monday, and we're supposed to check out at noon. I don't want to scare Ginger."

Nurse Norma listened without interrupting. I'm sure it wasn't easy.

"Sir, newborn babies don't have the strength to hold their heads up. In fact, she won't be able to hold up her head by herself for months. Just like she can't eat birthday cake."

Nurse Norma showed immediate signs of guilt for her final comment. I'm sure it slipped in from pure frustration without evil intent. I had no idea before the birth of my child exactly how little I knew about children. I have no nieces or nephews. I never dated a woman with children, or if I did, I never paid them any attention. An entire segment of society had flown beneath my radar. All these baby people seemed to be part of a cult, like the strange folks who go see the movie *Rocky Horror Picture Show* over and over again. I never could figure them out.

I went ahead and signed the birth certificate papers

without a fight. The nurse made Ginger sign a "release form" ordering her to have six weeks of pelvic rest. Nurse Norma explained it this way, "Ginger, pelvic rest means no intercourse for six weeks."

Just for fun I said, "Now Norma, I don't think we can make it six weeks."

Neither of the women bothered to look at me. Ginger's parents arrived shortly thereafter, and we agreed I would go to my apartment to take a shower and the baby would go to Ginger's. Besides everything else, I wondered if Ginger's parents still believed I raped their daughter. Surely by now Ginger had told them the truth, whatever the hell the truth was.

I arrived at my home to find a large pile of dog shit as my welcome mat. My first thought was I had been left a calling card by Lida and the beast, but I had no proof, and simply stepped over the robust heap and entered my home. The phone was ringing.

"Hello."

"Barry Munday! Where have you been? It's Donald."

"I've been at the hospital. I had a baby."

"A baby. Holy shit. What kind of baby?"

"A girl baby."

"What did you name her?" he asked.

I hesitated. "Cornelia."

He hesitated. "Cornelia? O.K.," and then he continued. "What happened to you that night at the Beaver Tree?"

There was a knock on the door.

"Hold on a minute, somebody's at the door."

I walked across the room to find a sheriff's deputy

standing on the other side of the welcome mat.

He said, "You've got a pile of dog shit on your welcome mat."

"I'm aware," I said.

"Are you Barry Munday?"

"Yes, I am."

"I've got a court summons for you. Sign here."

"A court summons? What for?"

"You've been charged with cruelty to animals. Says here it happened just a few days ago. You must've made somebody important pretty mad. It usually takes weeks to process these things."

I signed where he told me to sign and stood at the door reading the summons. It was some sort of criminal complaint signed by Lida Griggs. There was a court date listed on the bottom for January.

Halfway through my shower I remembered Donald on hold. Too bad for Donald. I didn't want to talk to him anyway. He'd call back. Standing in the shower it seemed virtually impossible to get up and go to work the next day. I didn't get much sleep during the weekend. Maybe I could be a stay-at-home dad and Ginger could go back to her high-paying job. It occurred to me that I had no idea where she worked. Maybe her rich father would allow me to manage his investments in the stock market and be paid handsomely. I could set up a computer in Ginger's apartment and make stock trades with Cornelia on my knee. Surely she could refrain from crying for important matters like stock trading.

I drove to Ginger's apartment. There was a gigantic pink bow nailed on the door. As I raised my hand to knock, I heard the door of the apartment behind me open. I turned to see the head of a man, an Asian man, peering around the corner. Our eyes met, and he immediately closed the door, not loud, but swift. I imagined he stood peeking through the peephole watching my every move.

Was he the same man I saw standing in the lobby at the hospital? I couldn't be sure. Since the incident at the Beaver Tree I had learned to doubt my ability to recognize the human face, or any other feature for that matter. Was it just another odd coincidence? And why did he close the door so quickly?

I found a place in the middle of the big pink bow to knock. Ginger's mother opened the door with the baby in her arms. I could hear the shower in the back bedroom, and I was alone with Mrs. Farley for the first time. We danced the dance of people who have nothing to say. There was a fuzzy brown cat on the couch. I hate cats.

"Is that Ginger's cat?" I asked.

"Yes. She's had him since she was a little girl."

"What's it's name?" I asked.

"Gary."

"Gary?"

"Yes."

We exchanged the baby back and forth and our conversation rotated around our common axis, Cornelia. I decided to take advantage of this opportunity to gather information from Ginger's mother.

"Does Ginger have good neighbors?"

"Oh yes, they all seem to get along just fine. Mostly young people, students and young couples."

"Who lives across the hall?" I asked with a nonchalant

tone, pretending to pet Gary.

"He's a Chinese exchange student. They call him Moe. I think it's a nickname."

I thought, Moe, now that's a funny damn name. It's more of a sound than a name. I could crush Moe with one swing of my mighty American fist. I could bring him to his knees.

Mrs. Farley asked, "Do you like animals?"

My paranoia drifted like smoke through the cracks in my head. Could she possibly know of my recent charge of cruelty to animals? Could Lida Griggs and Jennifer Farley be childhood friends, conspiring in the back room of some grown-up sorority house, laughing and giggling over coffee and sweet rolls?

"Yes, I love animals."

Cornelia began to cry for no apparent reason. Her sounds reached supersonic pitch in a few short seconds. She went from totally asleep to highly agitated faster than I could think of the words and ask, "What's her problem?"

"She's hungry," Mrs. Farley explained.

"Why does she yell like that? Maybe she has colic."

"I don't think so," Mrs. Farley said harshly, like colic was a shameful disease. She took the baby in the back room for lunch. I went to the front door to sneak a look through Ginger's peephole. There he was, Moe I mean, leaning around his doorframe, waiting for something. His image through the peephole was distorted. It was hard to get a good look at the man.

With my eye to the hole, I said out loud, "Chinese bastard."

There was a noise behind me, and I turned to see Ginger, Mrs. Farley, and baby Cornelia.

"What did you say?" Ginger demanded.

"Nothing."

She pushed me out of the way and stuck her own beady little eye to the hole. Her eyeglasses rammed against the spot, glass on glass, and she lifted them on top of her head.

Ginger turned to me and said, "What is the matter with you?"

She had a point. What was the matter with me? Ever since the baby was born I'd felt a strange urge to protect and fortify, a primal desire to keep my baby and Ginger from harm and away from other alpha males. I suddenly felt very tired.

The baby had stopped crying. Apparently she wasn't hungry after all. I took secret pleasure in this fact and asked to hold the child. I sat on the couch as far away from Gary as I could sit. I've always heard cats will suffocate babies if they get the chance. I'm sure Gary's little mind was crazy with schemes and plans to catch Cornelia alone, undefended, another victim of the harmless family cat. I had reached the point of exhaustion where nothing made sense.

CHAPTER TWENTY-ONE

MUD BONANZA

Through some unspoken agreement I was allowed to sleep on the couch at Ginger's apartment. Every few hours the baby would cry like her hair was on fire, and we would get up and try new things to get her back to sleep. It reminded me of the times my car wouldn't start, and I'd do stupid things like shake wires in the engine or open and close the hood in blind attempts to make the problem go away.

Most of the time Cornelia was simply hungry. Screaming seemed an unacceptable form of communicating hunger. It would've been better if she just pointed to her mouth or rubbed her little belly. I, most certainly, wouldn't be allowed to go to McDonald's and stand in front of the counter screaming my bloody head off for a hamburger.

After staying up most of the night I would drive to my home each morning and get ready for work. It was hard to concentrate on the job, but I was driven by the idea that I had mouths to feed and a new college fund. Almost every afternoon after work I would go to the grocery store and build a stockpile of food and accessories for Ginger's apartment.

My relationship with Ginger took an interesting twist. The common bond of Cornelia and the seemingly overwhelming responsibility of our child fastened us together like two people screaming westward in a covered wagon through dangerous territory. Late at night, sitting together on the ugly brown couch, we started talking about ourselves. Sometimes sleep deprivation and pure boredom would lead us further than we intended to go.

One long night, about two weeks after the baby was born, we kissed. In the vast realm of sexual possibilities, it was small and unimportant. But in this universe we had created for ourselves, in Ginger's apartment in the middle of the night, with Gary curled up on the floor, and Cornelia finally asleep in her crib, it was a breakthrough of historical proportions. After all, they say it is the kiss that truly separates us from the animals. It is the most intimate of acts. Far more intimate than the physical gyration of intercourse. Long after the love has left a marriage, out of obligations and blind satisfaction, the husband and wife still copulate, heads turned away from one another. But the kiss is forgotten, a relic of the love once felt, like the bones of elephants around a dried-up lake bed.

We were talking on the couch. It was very quiet between words. I leaned over and just kissed her. It didn't last long, but she kissed back, and we both pretended it was normal despite the fact that it was anything but normal. After that day I gave her a kiss on the mouth each afternoon when I returned from work. Sometimes, when her parents or sister were present, the silly little kiss gave me a feeling of closeness that existed in the kiss itself without the confusion of distant expectations.

After Ginger's breast milk miraculously arrived, she began the complicated and strange process of pumping her breast milk into bottles. I was still very unclear about this procedure. I found myself alone in the apartment one Tuesday morning with the baby. I didn't have a meeting until lunch and decided to skip work that morning. Ginger and her mother went shopping. My curiosity drew me to the refrigerator, where I found a small bottle of breast milk on the top shelf between a red tennis shoe and a pair of black pumps. Out of fear of appearing stupid, I had avoided asking anyone in the Farley family about the location of Ginger's shoes.

I squeezed a drop from the bottle onto the palm of my hand. There was no smell, none at all, and the liquid was more watery than regular milk. I lifted my hand to my mouth and extended my tongue down toward the drop. I waited for the cool touch and forbidden taste, but instead, there was a loud unexpected knock on Ginger's front door. The shock caught my breath, and I scurried to the sink to wash the evidence from my hand. There were three more knocks, in a certain order just like the first three. Perhaps a code.

I peered through the peephole to see the big head of Moe, the Chinese exchange student across the hall. His head turned left, and then right, and then left again, nervous. He turned and walked across the hall to his open door and disappeared as it closed. I considered the possibility that Moe came over to Ginger's apartment every weekday morning after I left for work, with his secret knock and his bell-bottom jeans, teaching Cornelia Chinese words, and maybe even kissing the same lips I kissed each afternoon.

"Chinese bastard," I whispered.

Cornelia was sleeping soundly in her crib. I picked her up and took her to the bathroom mirror. I held her on my chest, lifting up her tiny head facing the mirror just below my own face. I turned our heads at the same time, slightly to the left, and then slightly to the right, upward just a bit, and then downward. There was a resemblance. It was there, in the chin and also in the forehead. We had the same forehead, that's for damned sure. Her hair was darker than mine, and her face was chubby and wrinkled, but there was something about Cornelia's chin that reminded me of my own chin. A good solid chin.

As I held the baby in the bathroom I had a brief rush of anxiety. Was I qualified to raise a child? People are required to pass a test to drive a car, or get a license to go fishing, but to bring a baby into this world, the biggest responsibility in life, and raise that child, there is no requirement to pass a test or get a license. Any idiot can donate seeds or eggs. That's the brainless part of the process. Now what? What if my child hates me, I thought? What if she can tell I'm not qualified? I looked down in the mirror to see Cornelia's little dark eyes watching us. Maybe she already knew everything she needed to know to survive. Through my hand resting on the baby's backside I felt a rumble down below and then an enormous fart exploded our moment of silence.

I remember Ginger's mother telling me before she left that the baby hadn't gone "number two" for three days. Ever since we started the formula supplement, the bowels had slowed. The baby was administered what was called a glycerin suppository, and I was warned of the possibilities. Now the possibilities had come to fruition. How bad could it be? A little bitty baby, on a liquid diet, how much poo could she produce?

I laid Cornelia down on her back on the changing

table. I unfastened the left side of the diaper, and then the right, slowly folding back the front of the diaper to reveal a mountain of mud-like feces. It was man-sized and smelly, covering every square inch of skin beneath the diaper. My gag reflex kicked up in my throat and I dry-heaved. The baby began to cry uncontrollably, shaking, mouth wide open, screaming for relief. I ran to the bathroom and wrapped a towel around my face just below the eyes covering my nose and mouth like a train robber. I wiped and wiped and wiped between heaves until I gave up and held the baby's bottom half under the shower until the brown enemy was gone away.

I dried Cornelia, laid her back down on the changing table, and hunted for a new diaper. I lifted the baby's legs to slide the new diaper into place and the volcano erupted once again. The tiny bowels moved with the determination of a locomotive, and I was dumbfounded by the sheer amount of poo stored inside my little child. If I had removed her head like a cookie jar and filled her up with gravy, I don't believe she could hold as much as my eyes had seen. The gag reflex returned, and we started all over again with the shower and diaper routine. Thank God Ginger had been brought to her senses and decided to accept the concept of the diaper as a necessary poison. Otherwise, I may have actually died.

Finally Cornelia was all wrapped up and warm. I was proud of my survival and hoped Cornelia would have no memory of the ordeal. As we sat together in the living room my mind wandered to the fear of my upcoming court appearance. I had decided not to tell Ginger or her family and hopefully slide quietly past the embarrassment.

As the date approached on the calendar my apprehension grew steadily.

Facing Lida was bad enough, but I also faced the legal uncertainty, the prospect of a conviction or a fine. I was prepared to rely upon the fairness and common sense of our American judicial system, tried and true, even Steven, due process, God bless America.

CHAPTER TWENTY-TWO

THE TRIAL

My court appearance was scheduled at 5:00 P.M. in the city court in the heart of New Orleans. I lied to Ginger and told her I had to meet a client after hours. She didn't question my story. Either she didn't have much experience being lied to, or she didn't give a shit. I felt guilty anyway. I almost wanted her to doubt me, to pull the truth out piece by piece and strangle me in my own deception. Instead, Ginger smiled and said, "I'll see you when you get here."

The courtroom was packed with people from every level and forgotten hole in the city. I took a seat in the back against the far wall so I could see everyone as they came through the big double doors. There were lawyers and cops and court people going from one place to another like it all made sense, but I knew better. Every few minutes a buxom middle-aged blonde would yell out the name of a case and people would step forward and stand before the judge. He looked about fifty, the judge I mean, on the heavy side, mostly gray hair. He moved and spoke like a man with confidence in his actions. The type of confidence that only comes from experience, years and years of experience, slowly dulling the importance and seriousness of the courtroom scene. The look in his eye said he'd heard it all a thousand times before. I watched him put people in jail without a twitch of sympathy in his voice.

I wore a nice shirt and tie. My sleeves were rolled up. Sitting near the front on the opposite side I recognized the two guys from the grocery store. One sat with his mouth hanging open as he watched the judge sentence a drunk lady to five days in jail for urinating on the streetcar. It wasn't her first offense.

I spotted Newton Creech among the lawyers to the side of the judge's bench. With his eyepatch he stuck out in the crowd like a pirate at a bar mitzvah. I slumped down in my seat and searched through the faces and the backs of heads for Lida. Newton Creech said something to the judge, and they both laughed. I was sure his presence in court had nothing to do with me.

I was in the process of hoping my case would be called late in the evening in front of an empty courtroom when the buxom blonde yelled, "Barry Munday—cruelty to animals—witnesses Lida Griggs, Tony Howell, and Barney Perkins."

I stood and walked to the front. A man in a gray suit, I assumed he was the prosecutor, positioned himself between me and the other witnesses. There was a low mumble from the crowd as Lida appeared from nowhere with the gigantic dog held tightly on a leash at her side. The audience went silent, sensing that perhaps this was a case worth hearing. My eyes caught the good eye of Newton Creech. He stopped in the middle of a conversation and moved closer to hear what was going on. The judge shuffled through some papers and asked, "Are you Barry Munday?"

I was nervous to the point of losing my breath. It hit me all at once as soon as I opened my mouth to speak. "Yes, sir," I managed to answer.

"Do you have a lawyer?"

"No, sir."

"Are you able to afford the services of an attorney?"

"I guess so, yes, sir."

The judge looked up at me for the first time, obviously not nervous at all, and we held a stare. I don't think he liked what he saw as I balanced between cocky and unconscious.

"How do you plead, Mr. Munday, to the charge of cruelty to animals, guilty or not guilty?"

"Not guilty, sir."

"Everyone who is going to testify, please raise your right hands."

In my nervousness I raised my left hand, put it down, and quickly raised my right so the oath would be official. I saw the other witnesses, including Lida, raise their right hands.

"Do you swear to tell the truth, the whole truth, and nothing but the truth, so help you God?"

"I do," we all answered in unison. Things seemed to be going well so far.

I remember bits and pieces of the trial. It's like an old film in my head, herky-jerky from frame to frame.

I heard Barney Perkins say, "We were just standin' there about one in the mornin', me and Tony, trying to figure out what kind of beer to get, and this dude here comes sneakin' out of the back of the grocery store, peekin' around the corners, lookin' for somethin', I didn't know what, and then the dog comes out, and the dude turns and throws a jar of baby food and hits the dog on his head."

"What did the dog do?" the prosecutor asked.

Barney Perkins said, "He stood up stiff, like Scooby-Doo on the cartoon, and then just fell over. The dude ran away with his big cake, and the dog laid there. I thought he was dead, man, you know as hard as he got hit, but that dog got up a few minutes later and staggered around. It was some crazy shit."

The judge interjected sternly, "That's enough, Mr. Perkins. Next witness please."

"Judge, the testimony of Mr. Howell would be repetitive. We'll call Lida Griggs."

Lida took one step forward toward the judge. She was wearing black leather pants and a weird tortoise-shell choker around her neck. Alongside the humongous Great Dane, Lida was stunning in a courtroom full of baboons.

She began, "Barry and I dated for seventeen months. The boys developed a very close bond during that period of time. I hate to admit it, but there were times I was actually jealous of their relationship."

I vaguely remember at this point wondering if I was dreaming again. Lida's face began to take on a hazy muted outline.

She said, "When he saw Barry in the grocery store that night down the aisle, he just couldn't wait. He took off, and I was shocked to see Barry run like we were strangers."

She stopped for a moment and her face changed. Lida looked directly at the judge and said, "Barry Munday hates my dog because he still has his balls."

There was a gasp from the audience.

"Whose balls?" the judge asked.

"His own balls," I heard Lida say.

This had to stop. I raised my hand slightly and said, "Your Honor, how can this possibly be relevant to the case?"

The judge answered, "I'm not sure, Mr. Munday, but it sure is interesting."

There was a burst of laughter, and I was quite sure everyone in the world was insane.

"Continue please, Ms. Griggs," the judge said.

Lida looked at me and said, "I've got veterinarian bills of eleven hundred dollars. You gave him a concussion."

"A concussion," I said. "How do you know? He's got a skull like a freakin' mammoth."

Very calmly the judge said, "Mr. Munday, if you speak out of turn once more, you'll go to jail for contempt. Do you understand?"

I apologized, "Yes, sir. I'm sorry. I'm not a lawyer. I don't know all the rules."

"That's why you hire a lawyer, Mr. Munday, so you can be represented by someone who knows the rules. Have you ever heard the old saying, 'A man who represents himself in court has a fool for a client'?"

Things weren't going well. I looked at Newton Creech, and he looked at me. The visual image of his milky white eye appeared in my mind for no good reason.

I heard the judge say, "Mr. Munday, why don't you tell me your side of the story?"

I took a deep breath and prayed the words would come.

"Judge, the dog hates me. He came after me full speed down that grocery store aisle, and I ran. He chased me through the storage rooms and eventually back out into the store. That's the reason I was sneaking around. I was trying to get out of the store alive."

I paused, and started again, "He busted through the doors after me. I just panicked. I pulled the jar from my pocket and threw it. I had no idea it would hurt the dog. I just wanted him to leave me alone. And besides, there's no way I gave that animal a concussion. How can we tell anyway? His head's like a brick."

When I finished there was complete silence, like a church after a bad sermon.

The judge said, "Mr. prosecutor, do you have any questions for the defendant?"

"Yes, I do," he answered, and then asked, "Mr. Munday, you said you pulled the baby food jar from your pocket, correct?"

"Yes."

"Was that your pants' pocket?"

"Yes."

"Did you have other jars of baby food also in your pockets?"

"Yes, three or four. I dropped one in the storage room and put the others in my pockets."

"Had you already gone through the front register and purchased these jars of baby food or the cake you were carrying?"

"No," I answered slowly.

"So then, if you hadn't paid for the jars of baby food yet, but you had them stuffed in your pockets, were you trying to steal those items?"

I looked to the judge for help. He said, "Don't look at me, Mr. Munday. Answer the question."

I turned to the prosecutor, "Of course not."

The prosecutor said, "Well, let me get this straight. You're in a grocery store at 1:00 A.M., alone. You stuff your pockets full of baby food in the storage room behind the store. And when you realize you're about to get caught because the dog is drawing attention to you, you throw one of the jars as hard as you can at the dog from just a few feet away and nearly kill the dog? All so you won't get caught shoplifting, correct?"

I turned to the judge and said quietly, "I know this doesn't look good."

He agreed, "No, Mr. Munday, it doesn't look good. In fact, I find you guilty of the charge of cruelty to animals. I order you to reimburse Ms. Griggs the amount of her veterinarian bills, pay the costs of court, and serve a night in our lovely downtown jail to think about what you did. And tonight's as good as any. Bailiff, could you escort Mr. Munday to the holding cell?"

I couldn't believe my ears. At the worst I imagined a fine, maybe community service, but not jail. Not handcuffs and veterinarian bills.

I spoke up, "Judge, I'm actually a decent person. This was just a weird situation. I'm not a criminal."

The deputy stepped forward and began to lead me away. The judge leaned up in his chair and said to me, "Mr. Munday, we are what we do. And that's all there is to it."

I should've hired a lawyer. I was led past Newton Creech to a back holding cell with all the other people going to jail. They sat me down next to the woman who urinated on the streetcar. I closed my eyes and waited for something good to happen.

CHAPTER TWENTY-THREE

A WALL OF STINK

"Where's Daddy?"

"Oh, he's in jail."

"What for?"

"He tried to kill his ex-girlfriend's dog with a jar of your baby-food at one o'clock in the morning in a grocery store on the day you were born."

The imaginary conversation took place in my head on the drive from the courthouse to the jailhouse in a big brown van. I half hoped Newton Creech would call Mr. Farley, and Mr. Farley would unleash his power to have me released immediately. The other half of me hoped Newton would keep his mouth shut so I could serve my time and preserve the secret of my life of crime.

I was fingerprinted, booked, photographed, and sprayed for lice. I stood naked with one hand over my eyes and the other hand over my shy genitalia, trying to imagine a more humiliating pose. The jail was less crowded than I had envisioned, and I was led to a jail cell I would share with one old man. The cell was small with a toilet against the back wall and only one bunk bed. The old man lay on the bottom bunk, bare-chested and wild-looking. His head and face were covered almost completely with long stringy gray hairs.

The old man asked, "Are you the doctor?"

"No."

"Then who the hell are ya?"

I shook my head, "That's a good question. I guess I'm

your roommate."

He pointed to the top bunk, and as I approached I ran smack into a wall of stink. The old man in his little nest smelled like rotten cheese. As I got comfortable on the top bunk my mind raced through the theories of physics and I remembered without celebration that heat rises. Stink is warm. You can't separate the warm air from the smell. They drifted upward together, inseparable, forming a brown cloud around my body.

The light in the room was on, and I could read the dirty messages scrawled on the wall. There was racket up and down the halls with an occasional howl. I'm not afraid to say I felt fear. It reminded me of the childhood fear I felt each time I moved up from my old school to the new school. It took months to learn that people were really the same. Luckily, there in jail, I knew I wouldn't have months to figure out the fear. Instead, I'd have one long sleepless night in a cell with the smelliest man who ever lived.

From down below I heard the old man say, "Can you smell me?"

"Yes, I believe I can."

"Do I smell good?" he asked happily.

I leaned my head over the edge of the bunk and looked down at the old man, nothing but bones and white skin and hair. He had a twitch, a convenient outward sign that something inside wasn't quite right.

"No sir, you don't smell good. In fact, if you want to know the truth, you smell worse than you'd smell if you were actually dead, if that's possible."

The old man rolled his nose under his armpit and took a sniff. He seemed pleased with what he found. Can crazy people make themselves believe a bad smell is good? I turned over on my bunk and stared up at the ceiling. Someone had managed to etch their name high above: BUFORD. I wondered if Buford would request the same cell every time he came to jail so he could look at his handiwork.

The old man said, "What are you in for?"

"It doesn't matter. I'll be out tomorrow, and it'll be like it never happened."

"That's what I said forty years ago, but I keep comin' back," the old man remarked.

There was a moment of silence and then the old man said, "You're the first girlfriend I've ever had."

I rolled back over so he could see my face. We stared at each other a moment too long and he said, "What are ya lookin' for down here?"

"Nothing," I whispered and assumed my position looking at the ceiling again.

Without encouragement the old man said, "I got arrested in the mall."

I listened. He began again, "I was walkin' around in the big mall keepin' my eye peeled for a good thing when I stumbled up on a fountain inside the mall. One of those fountains with a place to sit on the edge.

"Down on the bottom there was hundreds of shiny pennies. Hundreds. And some nickels and dimes and even a few quarters."

Somebody screamed down the hall, "Fuck you, Winston."

The old man started where he left off. "So I dug through my pockets and found me one old penny. I threw the penny in the water and made a wish."

There was a touch of anger in the man's voice. "Well hell, I wished I could have all the rest of them damn pennies, and nickels, and dimes. That's what I wished for.

"So I rolled up my pants and got in that fountain to make my wish come true. I had a pocketful when that mall cop walked up like he owned the place."

The old man switched to sadness and sounded like he would cry.

"He took all my damn pennies. Every single one. Even the penny I got from my own pocket, the lucky penny. Damn cop. Ain't got no right gettin' in the middle of a wish, especially one that's comin' true."

It was a crazy story by a crazy smelly man in a jail cell in New Orleans. I missed Cornelia and Ginger and that stupid cat, Gary. I imagined Moe was taking advantage of my absence and sitting down to a homemade meal in my chair in Ginger's apartment. Eventually I would be forced to have a final violent confrontation with Moe. It seemed inevitable.

The old man was sobbing. I could feel the bed shake. He stopped when a voice down the hall yelled, "I hate celery."

"Me, too," I said.

The old man asked, "What's your name?"

"Barry. Barry Munday."

Out of obligation I asked, "What's your name?"

The old man said, "Calvin."

My eyebrows raised. "Calvin what?" I inquired.

"Just Calvin," he said.

I asked, "No middle name? No last name?"

"No."

We were silent for at least one entire minute before I asked, "Do you know a person named Ginger Farley?"

"None of your damn business, little boy," he growled.

How many people in this world are named Calvin, I thought? And how many of these Calvins live in a one-hundred-mile radius of Ginger Farley? And how many of these Calvins in a one-hundred-mile radius don't have a middle name or a last name? Not many, I bet. What are the odds I would end up with one as a cell mate for my first and only night in jail? Not very good.

The old man finally fell asleep. I stayed awake the entire night. Newton Creech must have kept his pie hole shut. No one came to rescue me. It was just me, and the old smelly man, and the guy who hated celery, against the world.

At seven o'clock in the morning a guard appeared at the cell door. He said, "Munday! It's time for you to go home. The judge wrote on his order you get released at 7:00 A.M."

He looked at his watch and said, "It's 7:00 A.M., unless of course you'd like to stay a while longer with your new friend."

I could hear the old man scratch himself below me. His scratching must have released little molecules of odor sent floating like bubbles throughout the room. He was a giant scratch-n-sniff poster, and his smell existed as a separate entity prepared to survive alone if necessary.

I climbed down from the top bunk and stood at the door. As I was leaving, the old man said, "Knock, knock."

I turned and answered, "Who's there?"

He looked puzzled, but finally said with reservation, "Calvin. You know me. We're friends."

"Calvin who?"

The old man's head cocked to the side and his mouth pulled up in the corner. He finally smiled and said, "I get it. It's a trick question. You're a tricky son-of-a-bitch, aren't ya?"

I walked with the guard down the long hall toward freedom. I could hear the crazy old man laughing behind me. I changed clothes, received my few personal items, and walked outside to a bright new morning. Ginger sat on the hood of her old car reading a book. She casually looked up and said, "You need a ride to your car at the courthouse?"

I hadn't thought about it. "Yeah, I guess so."

We were riding along in a pleasant silence when Ginger said, "You smell strange."

There was no need for explanation, any explanation at all, about why I smelled strange, or struck the dog in the head with a baby-food jar, or had the jars in my pocket in the first place, or didn't know infants can't eat baby food, or cake, or celery, or any other damn thing anywhere in the universe. The time for explanations had passed.

Looking out the car window I said to myself, "Daddy's comin' home."

CHAPTER TWENTY-FOUR

A DROOLING, RABID, GOAL-ORIENTED PAVLOVIAN DOG

I stayed in the shower a long time scrubbing and scrubbing. I didn't trust my own nose. The warm water felt magnificent, and then for some reason I remembered the time I was eight years old and went sleepwalking. I woke up two blocks away from home in my pajamas in the middle of a winter night. I felt completely and utterly alone and lost. I didn't recognize anything and had no idea where I was. For all I knew, my mother was dead and I was on another planet, far away in space. It was horrible. For years I would stop the memory each time I started because I knew it would take me to that place again, knocking on the door of a strange house, being even more afraid when the face at the door was not my mother's face. It occurred to me that Calvin must feel such a feeling every day of his life. It's no way to live. He should have made a better wish. He shouldn't have wasted his one good wish, maybe the only good wish in his entire life, on a pocket full of shiny pennies.

My bathroom at the Guest House had a long full-length mirror on the back of the door. I stood and stared at my breasts. Ever since Newton Creech's comment about male lactation pills, I suffered from a fear my breasts were growing. I wondered if it could be a side effect of my operation. Had I forgotten to take my hormone pills every day? Or was I just getting old, out of shape, listless like a sloth? I turned left and then right in the mirror. Maybe that's why Calvin thought I was a woman. Maybe my tits are gigantic.

I arrived at work a half-hour late and stopped at Lucy's desk to collect my messages. We exchanged greetings, and I stood nearby as I thumbed through the stack of little blue papers. My eyes were so tired I could barely focus.

Lucy looked up and said, "What's that smell?"

I moved toward my office and said, "What smell? I don't smell anything."

I went directly to the bathroom and slathered myself with a generous handful of Lonnie Green's hidden stash of cheap cologne. Before I could get settled behind my desk, Lonnie Green himself poked his head around the door.

"Hey, Captain, got a minute?"

"Sure."

He closed the door behind him, a universal sign of an upcoming important conversation, and sat down across my desk.

Lonnie's face wrinkled. "What's that smell?"

"Which smell?" I asked, tired of the subject.

"Never mind," he said. "Anyway, I talked with Tom Farley yesterday. He's close, Barry, damn close. He acts like he wants to give us his business, the whole damn company. Lock, stock, and barrel. The whole kit and caboodle."

Lonnie squinted his eyes, leaned forward toward me, and stared. He finally said, "Are you wearing makeup again?"

"No, Lonnie, I'm not wearing makeup again. I don't

wear makeup. And I stink because I spent the night in jail with the smelliest man on the face of this Earth, and I covered myself with your cologne to hide the nasty smell."

We sat still. Lonnie Green looked at me for a moment, smiled, stood up, and pointed at me as he said, "You're a wild son-of-a-bitch, Barry Munday. Now make that sale."

His fingers clinched into a fist, and he said, "Take life by the balls, Captain." And then he stomped away. Nothing fazed the man, nothing. He was unshakable. A drooling, rabid, goal-oriented Pavlovian dog.

Ginger called a few minutes later to invite me to dinner at the Farley house that night. The remainder of the day was uneventful, and I drove from work directly to Ginger's apartment a little earlier than usual. I looked forward to the opportunity to catch Moe off guard. I was sure he was quite smart, being an exchange student and all, but I was smarter, and it was just a matter of time until the yellow devil learned his lesson the hard way.

The coast was clear in the hallway. Ginger let me in the apartment, and we performed the ritual kiss. I held on just a bit longer than usual and Ginger let it happen. I took Cornelia in my arms. She was bright, and alert, and her little dark eyes darted around the room, stopping on lights and movement.

"Did she sleep well last night?" I asked.

"No. She's got her days and nights mixed up."

In the flow of the conversation I asked, "By the way, I was thinking about moving closer. Does anyone still live in the apartment across the hall?" It was a multilevel trick question.

Ginger was in the kitchen. Her answer was a beat too

late. "I don't know," she said.

Ginger was coy. It added fuel to my irrational fire. Burn irrational fire, burn. Reach your leaping gold flames into the black night, twisting and churning with angry heat. I hadn't slept in nearly forty hours, and there was no relief in sight. With dinner at the Farleys looming in the headlights, I struggled to maintain my balance of reason.

We carried bottles and bags and blankets and baby paraphernalia. I wasn't in the Farley house thirty seconds when big Tom Farley motioned for me to meet him down the hall in his private office. If I hadn't been so tired, I would've been more afraid. The exhaustion was like whiskey.

I let him begin. "Ginger says you've been a lot of help with the baby. I don't mean just financially."

I listened. Mr. Farley continued, "Ginger told me the truth about you two. I don't like it, but it is what it is."

Curiosity got the best of me and I asked, "What part do you not like?"

It was a bad question, obviously bad. The big man's face grew stern.

"What the hell part you think, you little shit-eater."

There was that name again. Mr. Farley took a deep breath and said, "I've tried very hard with you, Barry. I really have. You crapped all over my bathroom and crawled out my window. I watched a crazy woman in a restaurant punch you in the gut at a business lunch. You accused Jennifer of being a stripper in front of our priest. You yanked off a man's eyepatch. And on top of it all, you got my daughter pregnant in some bizarre religious sexual ceremony. What's next, Barry? What?"

There was a long pause while I contemplated the meaning of "bizarre religious sexual ceremony." What the hell had Ginger told the man? What had I done? Was Ginger willing to make up another crazy story to avoid admitting to consensual sex?

We sat across the big mahogany desk from one another, and I tried to hold back a smile I knew would get the best of me. It was just too ridiculous. A bizarre religious sexual ceremony. What could it mean? I wished Calvin was in the room with us. He would know what it means. He's probably been to one.

My smile got out.

Mr. Farley leaned up in his chair again and said, "What's so damn funny? Tell me. I'd like to know."

I tried to sit up straight like a kid in school. "I'm sorry, Mr. Farley. The baby's been up all night, and I haven't gotten much sleep. I'm trying to work long hours, reach my goals at the office. The lack of sleep is making me a little crazy, but I don't wanna lose ground at work."

Lonnie Green would have been proud. I put my face in my hands and rubbed my eyes. In my mind I repeated, "concentrate, concentrate." Lonnie's words swam around, "Seal the deal. Grab life by the balls."

Mr. Farley spoke. "I've decided it's time my company switched insurance agencies. I want you and Lonnie to put together the deal. It's yours, Barry. Don't make me sorry." We stood and shook hands across the desk like men. One burden was lifted and immediately replaced by another burden, new and heavy, the burden of business. After the manly shake, I turned and walked to the door. Behind me Mr. Farley said, "I'll see you at the dinner table, Barry."

On the way down the hall I stepped into the bathroom and flipped on the light. In the mirror I saw dark half-circles under my droopy eyes. I lifted the seat as required and positioned myself over the toilet for a much-needed piss. I'm not sure whether it was a noise or a feeling, but something made me turn my head toward the shower and the closed curtain behind me. And then I saw Jennifer's face at the edge of the shower curtain watching me pee.

There was a shock, a physical knee-jerk reaction, and I pissed all over the floor and my pants before I could regain control. She pulled the curtain to the side in one swift yank and stood in the shower smiling. I zipped up.

"Jesus, Jennifer, what are you doing?"

"Guess," she said, in a low sexy voice.

I watched her unzip the back of her skirt and drop it to the shower floor. She slowly lifted her shirt above her head and stood before me in vivid white bra and panties. I wanted to leave. I knew it was a trap, but I simply couldn't physically disengage my eyes from her perfect body. I couldn't physically move.

Still smiling, Jennifer reached those long fingers around her back and unlocked the bra. It was soon gone, as were the panties Jennifer pulled down to her ankles and flipped away. She bent over, my favorite part, and picked up the pile of clothes and dropped them on the bathroom floor outside the tub. I was mesmerized. I wanted to taste and smell every square inch of her nut-brown skin.

Fully naked Jennifer said, "Listen."

Down the hallway a door opened and then closed. The sound of big Tom Farley's footsteps came down the hall and past the door as my heartbeat picked up pace.

Footsteps disappeared down the other end of the hallway.

Jennifer said, "Every night before dinner, Daddy leaves his office, walks down the hall, and sits at the head of the table in the dining room. As you might remember, the head of the table faces down the hallway directly to this bathroom door."

The situation began to come clear in my mind.

She whispered, "Mother and Ginger know I'm in here taking a quick shower."

Jennifer smiled, "By the way, what are you doing in here anyway, you dirty pervert?"

She turned the shower on and pulled the curtain closed. I was trapped. Soon Ginger and her mother would figure out I was no longer with Mr. Farley in his office. Soon Mr. Farley would notice I wasn't with Ginger and her mother. I couldn't risk leaving through the door, especially with the sound of the shower. I couldn't even risk opening the door. There was a moment, ever brief, when I considered stripping naked and getting in the shower with the goddess. It was the ultimate short-term plan.

I turned to my favorite window. It could work, I thought. Crawl out the window, run around front, act like I stepped out for a breath of fresh air. It was possible.

I opened the window quietly and peeked outside. All clear. I pulled myself up to the ledge with the sound of the shower behind me and began to crawl out the window into the prickly holly bush. There was a sudden flash of light and the click of a camera. I was temporarily blinded by the light and fell headfirst into the bushes. There was the sound of feet running away across the grass and over the patio.

Someone had taken my photograph as I was crawling out of the Farley bathroom window. Who? Who would do it? Who would wait in the shadows and take this picture? Mrs. Farley? No. Mr. Farley? Why? Ginger? Who was it? A neighbor? Newton Creech?

I gathered myself from the bush and closed the window before I ran around to the front door. I casually let myself in like a man back from a nighttime walk. Newton Creech had arrived and was sitting at the dinner table with Mr. Farley. No one gave me a second glance as I lifted Cornelia from her swing and entered the kitchen. Eventually everyone and the food ended up at the table. Jennifer, hair half-wet, appeared and sat down across the table from me.

She said, "Barry, is that a leaf in your hair?"

I touched the side of my head and fished out a crunchy brown leaf from my crispy hair. I looked at the leaf in my hand and tried to appear bewildered. Afterwards, as I ate, my eyes scanned the table. One of these people, I was sure, just minutes earlier, had stood outside with a camera and taken my picture as I was crawling from the bathroom window. I looked for clues in their eyes, but mostly I concentrated on making all the necessary efforts to preserve the visual image in my memory of Jennifer standing naked in the shower, unashamed and glorious.

CHAPTER TWENTY-FIVE

CRACKS IN MY SOLE

I know it sounds horrible, but in the first few months it was very difficult to establish any bond with my baby. There was a very obvious bond between Ginger and Cornelia, but I couldn't quite find the groove of father-hood. She was just a loud, smelly, wiggly little person demanding undivided attention and staring at something unseen across the room. I couldn't figure it out. But at two months, life began to change again. Those little eyes opened wide and watched me move across her vision. And then she smiled. It was like watching a flower bloom. Actually, it was like being the flower. I felt myself open.

Who knows if she meant to smile? Who cares? After that day I started to miss her like I've never missed another human being since I was a boy. I missed her little bitty hands and that round smushed-up face. I would rush to Ginger's apartment from work and hold the baby in my lap making clownish noises and faces like a babbling dork, all for a smile. One simple smile. And then I would lean back on the couch like an opium smoker, resting in a warm pool of satisfaction, feeling my priorities slipping gently into place.

Slowly but surely my personal items began to migrate to Ginger's apartment. The transition went unspoken. In fact, some of our best decisions together were made without a hint of discussion. Many times, sitting with her in the evening, I toyed with the idea of asking Ginger about the "bizarre religious sexual ceremony." But if I asked her I knew it would be a confession to my total lack of memory of our act of conception. I also reminded myself that Ginger's first story to the parents consisted of my slipping a Mickey Finn into her drink and quenching my manly desires on her plump lifeless body. Perhaps she had something to hide. Or perhaps Ginger herself had no memory of our drunken love session. Or perhaps the girl would rather concoct crazy-ass stories instead of admitting to her parents that she had unencumbered intercourse with a complete stranger like me. After I mulled it over two or three thousand times, it became hazy and unimportant, like a ball of lint from the dryer. Besides, maybe the truth was worse than the lies.

I began to visit my little apartment at the Guest House less and less, choosing to shower and dress at Ginger's place each morning. On one of my rare visits home I spotted something pinned to my door as I climbed the stairs. My eyes focused on the item on the door as I walked closer until I could see it was a photograph. I stood a few inches away and looked at myself in the picture climbing through the bathroom window of the Farley home. My ass was half-in and half-out balanced on the windowsill with my face straight ahead at the camera, eyes wide open like a madman. In the background through the window I could see the nude body of Jennifer with the shower curtain pulled back, one hand pointing toward me and her face with no expression. She must have stopped and watched me escape at the moment the camera flashed, and my image was forever captured on film climbing through the window of a naked girl's bathroom. Not just any naked girl. Ginger's sister. Tom Farley's baby daughter. The baby daughter he probably held on his knee so many years ago and begged to smile.

As I examined the picture on the door, a smell floated to my nose. I looked down to see my shoe resting squarely on a fresh pile of dog shit at my doorstep. The calling card of Lida. Could she be the photographer lurking in the bushes? Was it pure satanic luck that Lida would catch me exiting a bathroom window? Could I have been correct in my suspicion that Lida and Jennifer were linked in a conspiracy to drive me to the bat farm?

I removed my shoe and held it in the shower washing away disgusting bits of feces from the cracks in my sole. I finally just dropped the shoe in the shower and left it running. I located a bottle of 409 to clean up the mess on the doorstep. Back at the front door I found my landlord, Louis, standing with his hands on his hips and a scowl on his thin face.

"This is twice, Barry. Twice I've walked past your door to find a pile of excrement. Do you have a dog in there?"

"No, Louis, I don't have a dog. Somebody else's dog apparently likes my doorstep."

I bent down with paper towel in hand to grasp the pile. Through the thin paper I could feel the soft rancid consistency squeeze through my fingers as if there was no paper towel at all. I felt my stomach heave and my mouth open as I turned and ran to the toilet.

When I returned to the front door Louis had inched forward and was craning his ferret-like neck staring at the picture still pinned to the door. In my haste to wash the shoe I had forgotten to remove the photograph. It was too late.

Louis stood back like he was suddenly afraid of me.

"Mr. Munday, I want you outta here," he said. "You're not welcome to live here anymore. This is a Guest House, and as you know, you and Emma Howard are the only permanent guests. Families stay here, children. They visit from all over the world. It isn't healthy."

Wearing a single shoe, a bottle of 409 in one hand and a fresh paper towel in the other, I listened to the man at the door. His eyes kept sneaking back to the photograph.

"It isn't healthy," he repeated.

I took a deep breath, laced with stench, and said, "O.K., Louis, but if I have to leave, I don't see much point in cleaning up the rest of the dog shit. Do you?"

I handed the man the 409 and the fresh paper towel, removed the photograph, closed the door, and began to pack all my worldly possessions still left in the room. I was surprised to see how little I had accumulated in my lifetime. I could hear Louis outside the door, with his feminine sighs, scrubbing and spraying away the un-healthy dog shit. It made me smile. It was time for me to go anyway. Louis was right, and he didn't even know why.

I arrived at Ginger's apartment with my big brown suitcase and a few hanging clothes. There was no sign of Moe, but I secretly hoped he was seeing me through his peephole. Ginger answered the door with the baby in her arms. Without explanation I walked through the living room to my designated closet. The act of hanging my clothes solidified the fact that we were now officially living together, without the benefit of marriage, in separate beds, but living together nonetheless.

I walked to the kitchen, found a Budweiser in the

refrigerator behind a brown hiking boot, and sat down on the couch prepared for anything.

CHAPTER TWENTY-SIX

THE YELLOW MENACE

Lonnie Green was so excited about Tom Farley's business he could barely keep his pants on. Suddenly I was the golden boy with the golden touch. There was no time to read newspapers or go to imaginary meetings, even important imaginary meetings. I had to arrive at the office at seven o'clock in the morning just to catch up from the day before. Lonnie Green was always there ahead of me. We met at the coffee pot early one day.

"Mornin', Hot Shot. How's that baby doin'?"

"Good. She's good."

"What's her name again?" Lonnie asked for the first time.

"Cornelia."

"Cornelia?" he repeated. "Cornelia what?"

Even though I'd had this conversation with people a thousand times since the baby was born, I still hadn't figured out how to explain it away.

"Just Cornelia," I mumbled.

"What?"

"Just Cornelia. There's no middle name. No last name. Her name is just Cornelia."

Lonnie sipped his coffee and said, "Hell, ain't nothin' wrong with that. Caesar only had one name. Lassie… Madonna…Buddha. Lots of people with just one name."

"And Calvin," I added, patiently waiting for a response.

Lonnie Green took another sip from his favorite

coffee cup. The mug had a picture of huskies and a sled. Written above the huskies it said, "IF YOU AIN'T THE LEAD DOG, THE SCENERY NEVER CHANGES."

Lonnie took a second sip and said, "Yeah, Calvin," before he turned and walked away. Lonnie hated to feel left behind in a conversation. I learned the Calvin comment was the only successful defense when I found myself explaining my child's single name.

When the office opened at 8:30, Donald was waiting at the door. Lucy sent him back to my office.

"Hey, Barry. Long time no see," he said.

He seemed different. Donald's hair was longer, and it didn't suit him well. He sat down in the client chair across from my desk. His words were slow and bland.

"How's your baby? What's her name?"

"Cornelia," I answered with confidence, ready to pounce on the next question.

"That's a good name," Donald said, and then followed with, "I'm getting another divorce."

It was the first time I felt sorry for Dumb Donald. He looked bad.

"What happened?"

"She's crazy, man. Crazier than all the rest of 'em put together. In fact, she's like a big combination of every woman I ever hated. Or at least every woman who ever hated me. She burned my underwear."

"What?"

"She burned my underwear," he said again.

"Why?"

"I don't know. She just went around the house, gathered up every single pair, piled 'em in the bathtub, soaked 'em with lighter fluid, and lit 'em on fire. Set off the damn smoke alarm."

I tried not to smile. "Were you there?" I asked.

"No. I got home and the fire trucks were in the driveway."

We sat together for a moment. Dumb Donald stared down at the front of my desk. Finally he said, "You wanna go somewhere and get drunk? Maybe we could find out where those midgets are gonna be. They were damn funny, those midgets, especially that big one. You remember?"

"Yeah, Donald, I remember."

He was nowhere. Donald's life had stopped moving. I could see it in his eyes. Blank.

He said, "Those crazy brothers, Toby and Elvis, are gonna kick my ass. I know it. They think I cheated on their sister."

"Did you?" I asked.

"Not really."

We were quiet again. I felt like his big brother. It seemed important for me to say something important.

"Donald, you know what's the best thing that ever happened to me?"

He looked up from the desk. "What?"

"Losing my balls." I hesitated and then continued, "I know it sounds weird, but before that day, and really before I got the letter about the baby, my life was nowhere. I was in a hole. And then everything started moving, slowly like a big train leaving a station, taking me somewhere. Until that day, I had no idea how lost I was. I'll be the first to admit I didn't have much to do with getting that train started, and God knows I don't have any idea where it's going, but Donald, at least it's moving. I like my job now, and I can't wait to get home and see my baby."

There was quiet again.

Donald said, "You lost your balls?"

In my excitement to give advice, I had forgotten Donald didn't know about the incident.

"That's not important, Donald. The rest of what I said is important. All the stuff about the train, and life. That's the important part."

Donald's left eye twitched slightly and he asked, "Are we gonna get drunk together or not?"

I answered politely, "No, Donald, we're not."

He looked disappointed. Donald said, "Well, I've got to go. She said yesterday all my things would be in the front yard. I've got to go buy some underwear. Where's a good place to buy underwear? I've been wearin' this pair for two days."

Donald hesitated and added, "Why do they call it a pair of underwear anyway? There's just one."

I stood up to shake his hand, hoping he would leave. From his chair Donald said, "What's the deal with the breasts?"

"What do you mean?"

"It looks like you've got boobs, man," and he reached out to touch my chest. I pulled away and looked down at myself.

"I'm just outta shape, Donald. I don't have boobs."

Donald shrugged his shoulders, "O.K., don't freak out."

"I'm not freakin' out. I've got work to do. Good luck with your underwear."

He finally left my office. I stood behind my desk for a minute and stuck my chest out and then back in. They weren't really boobs, just bulges. I vowed to exercise.

Ginger called to ask if I could leave work a few hours early to watch the baby while she kept a doctor's appointment. I arrived home around three o'clock and took Cornelia in my arms. Almost an hour after Ginger left, there was a knock on the door. Through the peephole I could see Moe's round Chinese head. I looked down at Cornelia's head, and then back through the peephole at Moe. I held the baby up next to the peephole so I could look at her and then back at Moe a few times. The moment had come to confront the yellow menace. I swung open the door and we stood face to face.

"Moe, my name is Barry Munday. I live here now." It was the verbal equivalent of a dog marking his territory. The adrenaline rose in my blood, and my heart pounded beneath my masculine chest.

Moe spoke, "Sowwy. Is Geenja hum?"

He was a little man with a red T-shirt and oversized blue jeans.

"Why don't you come inside, Moe. We'll wait for Geenja together."

The little man was hesitant. Perhaps he sensed a trap, but he stepped inside anyway and sat down at the end of the couch closest to the door. I stood holding the baby in front of him. I noticed his dark eyes wouldn't look directly at me. They were focused a few feet to my right. I moved a few feet to the right and the eyes shifted farther right. I was unsure if he was intentionally avoiding eye contact, or if he had some type of vision disorder. I moved again slightly to my right, and again the dark eyes shifted. If I kept going it seemed I could eventually circle the entire room and end up back where I started.

"What's your problem, Moe?" I demanded.

"Pwobwum?"

"Yeah, pwobwum. Why you always sneaking around here, knocking on doors, lurking? What's your deal?"

Again I moved a few feet to my right, almost to the far end of the couch. Moe's eyes slid farther away. He looked nervous and probably wished he had trusted his instincts and stayed outside in the breezeway, a safe distance from the security of his dirty little home across the hall.

Without warning, the Chinese man sprung to his feet and ran for the door. He was agile and quick, moving with great purpose.

I yelled, "Don't come back, you little bastard," and he was gone, door slammed shut behind him, leaving me and Cornelia across the room. I ran to the door with the baby bouncing in my arms and stuck my eye against the peephole just in time to see Moe's door close with a bang. As I continued to watch, my mother's face appeared in the lens. I opened the door before she knocked.

"Hi, Mom."

"Who was that Chinese boy running away?"

"Oh, he lives across the hall."

"What did you do to him?"

"Nothing."

"Well, he sure was in a hurry. He ran smack into the wall next to his door."

"Which side?" I asked.

"What?"

"Which side of his door did he run into?"

"The left side."

"That figures," I said.

My mother took Cornelia from my arms and immediately started talking that female goo-goo baby talk.

"Mother, the child will never learn to speak good English if you talk to her that way all the time."

"You did," she said. "And I talked like this to you until you were ten years old." She was defensive.

"That explains a few things," I added.

Mom went to the refrigerator and removed a baby bottle with formula. Ginger had grown tired of the miracle of breast-feeding and the baby was on a pure formula diet.

"Mom, did you see any shoes in the refrigerator?"

"Yes," she said as she positioned the baby on her lap on the couch and began the afternoon feeding. I waited for her to add an explanation about the shoes, but instead she started back with the goo-goo talk. I changed the subject.

"Do you think Cornelia looks like me?"

Without lifting her head my mother said, "Yes, I do."

"Does she look like my father?"

My mother looked up. "No, she doesn't, and neither do you. Your father was a very ugly man." She looked down again.

It was the most information I had ever received about the man who was my father. As a child, through the years, I remember making a list of questions to ask my mother about him, and a separate list of questions to ask my father directly. The lists were long.

My mother, still looking into the eyes of the baby, said, "Boy, there ain't nothin' back there. Everything in this world is here now. Stop rooting around with your face in old corners. If you don't pay attention, it'll all disappear, and there won't be anything left but old corners. Now tell me what you did to the Chinese boy."

CHAPTER TWENTY-SEVEN

TACOS, POP-TARTS, STRAIGHT LINES, AND CHUNKS OF GOLD

On a crisp February Saturday morning Ginger and I had a small argument. She was right, I didn't do my fair share of diaper changes. I just wasn't good at it. Poo always ended up all over me, and the baby, and any item within a radius of three feet. If I was holding the baby, and felt a rumble down below, I tried to hand her off casually to the nearest woman and formulate a believable excuse. I think Ginger figured it out.

"Hey, I need to go to the bathroom. Could you hold the baby?"

"Not this time, Mr. Slick. You know where the diapers are."

"No, really, I've got to go to the bathroom," I pleaded.

Ginger mocked, "No, really, I was a little drunk and she was dressed like a rabbit."

I tried not to smile as I carried Cornelia to her changing table and laid her down. I retreated to the kitchen and tied a red bandana around my nose and mouth.

"I'm goin' in. If I'm not back in five minutes, call Nurse Norma." Ginger laughed. For some reason I noticed she wasn't wearing her glasses.

"Where are your glasses?" I asked.

Ginger's face squeezed tight like a cat. She said, "I got contact lenses over a month ago, and you haven't noticed. Would you notice if I had no head?"

Through the red bandana I mumbled, "Probably,"

and headed to the back room to face the diaper, which suddenly didn't seem so bad.

We planned to take the baby in her stroller across the street to the mall. Between Ginger's apartment complex and the mall was a busy four-lane highway. As the three of us approached the highway, me pushing Cornelia, I began to feel an odd tightness in my chest. The cars on the roadway were whizzing back and forth in both directions at great speed. At fifty yards away I felt lightheaded, and at twenty yards from the intersection there was hyperventilation.

"Ginger, I think maybe we should go back and drive to the mall."

"Don't be stupid, it's right across the street."

We stopped on the sidewalk next to a small house on the corner. The thought of crossing the road with the baby brought a sickness to my stomach.

"Please, Ginger, we should drive."

"It's a beautiful day," she said, and took hold of the stroller, moving toward the highway.

I closed my eyes, but the feeling wouldn't go away.

"What's the matter with you?" Ginger asked.

I took three deliberate steps toward a group of bushes, bent over at the waist, and threw up against the wall of the little house next to a window. I heaved once, and then twice, as the sound of a large truck filled my ears. After the third heave, obviously empty, I looked up to see a gray-haired lady in a nightgown standing at the window watching me upchuck. She was eating a Pop-Tart. I turned and walked back to where Ginger stood with Cornelia.

I cannot explain it other than to say the highway and

the speeding cars made me feel a total lack of control. It must be how a bear feels when the baby bears are in danger, although it's hard to imagine how vomiting could contribute to the survival of the young. I felt helpless, unable to protect my child. Ginger thought it was funny. She thought it was funny all day, laughing from time to time as we walked through the mall. Once we were across the street, all was well. Anxiety free.

I learned Ginger wasn't much of a shopper. We bought big cookies and watched Cornelia's eyes look at things for the very first time.

We were strolling along when I heard my name, "Barry! Barry." I heard it again, "Barry." And there he was, that crazy smelly old man from jail, Calvin, with his pants rolled up to his knees, barefoot, standing in the fountain in the middle of the mall.

"Barry, it's me, Calvin."

Ginger liked the whole damn thing. She turned the stroller and led us toward the fountain. There was a familiar musty smell.

Calvin was wearing a brown ski cap. His bushy gray hair and beard covered almost all the skin of his face and neck. The sleeves of his jacket around his hands were soaking wet and dripping.

The old man whispered, "Look. Money. There's money in here. I found a quarter." He held up a quarter and looked at it himself to be sure it was really there. He bit it like an old-time prospector biting a chunk of gold. People watched him as they passed, sometimes positioning themselves between the man in the fountain and their children.

I leaned toward Calvin and said, "You've got to get out of the fountain. You're gonna get arrested again. Remember what happened last time?"

"Oh hell yeah I remember. The last time I made a mistake. The last time I wished for all the money in this here fountain. This time I wished I was invisible. Now I can just take all the money, and when I'm done, there won't be nothin' left but a ripple in the pool."

The old man smiled, revealing a set of rotten teeth.

Ginger said, "I don't believe we've been introduced."

Reluctantly I said, "Calvin, this is Ginger. Ginger, this is Calvin."

The old man leaned over and fished out a silver dime. He said politely to Ginger as he rose, "Me and Barry dated a while in college. Is that a problem?"

"Really?" Ginger answered. "No, it's not a problem."

To put an end to the conversation I said, "Calvin, you're not invisible. I can see you as plain as day."

A big smile formed on his hairy face as he said, "Yeah, but I can't see you." He continued, pleased with himself, "You ain't so smart, you know. You don't even get the trick. You're like those people who think the world is flat. The world ain't flat, it's a straight line, from here to wherever you want it to go."

Calvin bent down and picked up a penny. He placed it on his tongue and swallowed it whole. I noticed Cornelia in her stroller sound asleep. She was unaffected by the insane man in the fountain, and I began to feel the same sickness I felt by the highway.

As I turned to leave Calvin said, "Hey, Barry, if you were all alone for the rest of your life in a wooden box, and all you had was a penny, what would you do?" And then for no reason the old man turned angry. He said, "Leave me alone. Don't call here anymore."

"O.K.," I answered, and we walked toward the food court, leaving the old man behind. I wanted to yell, "If you can't see me, then how do you know I'm Barry?" But it seemed a waste of time. You can't back a crazy man in a corner. There are no walls.

Between my first and second taco I had a thought. Where had I put the photograph from the front door? Between the dog shit, getting kicked out of the Guest House, packing, and moving into Ginger's apartment, I had lost track of the photograph. I couldn't remember where I put it, and God help me, I hoped it wasn't in a place for Ginger to find. I had already used my only chance at the amnesia explanation, and I certainly couldn't expect anything like the truth from Jennifer.

I took very deep breaths on the walk home and made it across the highway without a hitch. The old lady in the window watched us go by like we were on the silver screen. We reached Ginger's apartment, and she was the first to spot the fresh pile of dog feces at her doorstep. It was a new experience for her.

"Gross. That's disgusting. Look at that," she pointed.

I said, "Well, that's quite a pile for Gary the cat."

"That's not from Gary. That's dog shit." She was pissed off.

"Maybe you're right," I said, realizing that perhaps Lida had tracked me down.

I heard a scratching sound behind Moe's door across the hall. Ginger and I turned at the same time. There was a muffled bark, and then another. The sound of bare feet on linoleum.

I said, "It looks like your old friend Moe has a dog."

She seemed puzzled. "He never had a dog before."

I maneuvered Cornelia's stroller around the pile as we all three went inside to safety. I went through my dirty clothes, my luggage, the pockets of my pants and shirts, and even my shoes. No photograph. I crawled on my hands and knees looking under the bed, the dresser, the changing table, and behind the toilet. No photograph. Where could it be? Had she found it already and kept quiet? Not possible. I went outside to look in the car, and the trunk, and walked back and forth across the parking lot retracing my steps. I dug through the trash, trying to remember if I had taken it out in the last few days. No photograph. I went back to the same places to look two and three times hoping it would miraculously appear, which it didn't do. I visualized the photograph and tracked it in my mind from the door to my hand, from my hand to somewhere, and from somewhere to somewhere else. I did know one thing, there would be hell to pay if Ginger found the picture. Maybe I could call it a bizarre religious sexual ceremony.

CHAPTER TWENTY-EIGHT

A SEMICIRCLE OF DYSFUNCTION

Apparently my mother and Ginger Farley somehow formed an unholy alliance based at least partly on their common concern for my mental well-being. I had no idea of the existence of this alliance until I arrived at Ginger's apartment late one evening to find six strange men gathered in a semicircle in the living room. I stood in the doorway dog-tired and waited for an explanation. My mother and Ginger hovered near the kitchen counter.

A middle-aged man in a blue sweater stood from his chair near the couch and said, "Barry, my name is Preston Edwards. Please don't be alarmed."

The other five men smiled from their positions in the semicircle across the couch and in situated chairs. I turned to my mother, but she and Ginger had their eyes glued to Preston Edwards. He spoke again in the same calm voice.

"Your mother and Ginger are concerned about you. They love you very much."

I waited.

He continued, "They've seen a change in you since your injury in the theater."

I was still clueless.

"Barry, I'm a psychiatrist. Our group meets once a week to provide support to each other and help understand what has happened to each of us. I formed this group eight years ago after my own personal accident. Each of us, each of the men in this room, has experienced some type of genital mutilation or deformity."

I tried to hold my face without expression. It was too early to react. The man walked toward me, held out his hand to shake, and led me toward the group like a zombie. He gently closed the door behind, cutting off my escape route. On the edge of my vision I saw my mother and Ginger disappear into the back bedroom. My mother's mere presence clouded the possibility that the entire event was a joke, but the possibility still remained.

A chair was placed next to Preston Edwards, Dr. Preston Edwards, and I sat down. I felt like a hamster at show-and-tell.

The man explained, "Barry, our group is affiliated with the American Association of Genitalia Abnormalities, or A.A.G.A., as we like to call it. Every man in this room knows how you feel right now. Anger and confusion are common reactions to a surprise intervention."

I still hadn't spoken, and I didn't plan to. Looking around the room at the faces, I doubted seriously any man in the room had the slightest idea how I felt.

Preston Edwards said, "When we have a new member, we like to start the meeting by having each member stand and tell a little about themselves. We'll start with Bart and go from left to right."

A big red-headed country boy stood and said, "My name is Bart Winfield. I'm twenty-seven years old. When I was seventeen I had my genitals mutilated in a tractor accident. I've been in the group almost five years." He sat down.

Before I had time to think about Bart, the next man stood from his place at the end of the couch. He was tall and skinny, well-dressed, holding a book in his hands.

"My name is Kyle Pennington. I'm thirty-four years old. I have a master's degree in education. My penis is sixteen inches long, thin like a rope, and my testicles are the size of peanuts. I have a rare chromosomal defect known as Glassroth Syndrome. I am a founding member of the group."

I laughed. It couldn't be helped. I was surrounded once again by pure insanity, a semicircle of dysfunction.

The voice of Preston Edwards deepened as he said, "Barry, if you're laughing out of nervousness or embarrassment, that's understandable, but there's nothing funny about Kyle's condition. Our genitals are a large part of our identity, who we are. It's no less traumatic to have your genitals disfigured than it would be to have your face burned or scarred. Research indicates that the emotional healing concerning mutilation of a person's genitals is more difficult than any other injury."

Kyle Pennington frowned at me. It was impossible to look at the man and not form a visual image of his dangling rope-like penis with two Spanish peanuts stuck to the base almost buried in the curly jungle.

Preston nodded his head and the third man stood, hands tightly at his sides. He was short and bald with one blue eye and one brown.

"My name is Jerry Sherman. When I was eleven years old my penis was completely severed by a knife. The end barely pokes out like a turtle head, and I sit down to urinate."

"A turtle head?" I asked, speaking my first words of the evening.

"Yes, but my testicles are intact," Jerry Sherman

explained, and sat down in the middle of the couch.

Turtle heads and peanuts, I thought. There were two men left. I was on the edge of my chair.

A very small older black man stood. He wore a brown suit and tennis shoes. "My name is Lester Bidwell. One of my balls is below my pecker, and one of my balls is above my pecker. They ain't never seen each other."

Lester Bidwell sat down and then jumped back up. "Oh, this here is my third meeting, by order of the court." He grinned, and settled back into the warmth of the couch. He seemed proud of his genital abnormality as opposed to the other sad-sacks splashing around in self-pity and bitterness.

The last guy stood, turned his back to the circle, and began to speak. "My name is Maury Knox."

Dr. Preston Edwards interrupted, "Maury is a new member of the group. He prefers to speak with his back to us."

There was a moment of silence as Maury mustered the courage to continue his rehearsed speech. He repeated, "My name is Maury Knox. I have no genitals at all. My private spot is smooth and hairless. This is my second meeting." He turned back around and sat down.

During the introductions I had made no decisions on what to do next. I heard Cornelia cry in the back room and wondered how my mother and Ginger had ever found these people who were unable to forge a path in life beyond the loss of the special friends in their pants.

Dr. Preston Edwards said, "Barry, I know this is strange to you."

I blurted out, "It's not so strange. I worked hard all

day. I came home to see my baby, maybe have a beer. Instead, I opened the door to find six strangers sitting in the living room waiting to tell me stories about their genitals. It's perfectly normal, don't you think?"

Even Kyle Pennington looked at me with encouragement, excited to witness with his own eyes such a quick psychological breakthrough.

I leaned forward like we were in a football huddle and said, "Maybe, just maybe, we could combine all our private parts together and form one average set of balls and penis, and then we could rejoice and face the world as a single person, standing in front of a mirror pointing at our normal tallywacker. What do you think? Who's with me?"

Lester Bidwell said, "Hell yes."

My eyes darted from one man to the next. Dr. Edwards said calmly, "I understand, Barry. These things take time."

I attacked, "No, they don't take time. You take time. Too much time."

"We'll leave now," Dr. Edwards said. "I'll call you in a few days, and we'll talk about the next meeting."

The men stood quietly and walked out the door single file, Dr. Preston Edwards leading the way and Lester Bidwell lagging behind. When the door closed I walked to the refrigerator. There was a beer hidden next to a jar of pickled pears behind a single white pump. I popped the top, and a few seconds later the bedroom door cracked open. My mother and Ginger came out with the baby. They looked around the room for signs of the group.

My mother whispered, "Where did Dr. Edwards go? Did they leave already?"

I sipped my beer and then said, "Yes, Mother, they left."

She raised her voice to a normal level and asked, "What did you say to them? They were very nice men, except that Mr. Pennington, he gives me the creeps."

"Mom, if you had any idea what lives in that man's pants, you'd never let him in the house again."

Mother turned on me, "Don't be crude, Barry. Why can't you just let the people help you? I saw a documentary on television about a man who had his thing cut off. He had trouble from it, mental trouble. You should just be glad you got people in this world who care enough to try to help. It was Ginger's idea."

Ginger got involved. "Excuse me?"

The foundation of the alliance shook, and then my mother said, "Well, you know what I mean."

Yes, I did, but Ginger didn't. Later, when my mother left, I shattered the secrecy code of the A.A.G.A. and told Ginger about each of the men in the group. We laughed until we cried, which was more therapeutic than fifty meetings looking at the back of Maury Knox's head while he described his smooth marble-white pubic region.

CHAPTER TWENTY-NINE

TWO MEN AND A JAR OF URINE

After my encounter with the A.A.G.A. I began to actually wonder if it would do me good to join the group. There were so many unanswered questions in my life, about Cornelia and Ginger, and my father, and yet I felt no motivation to ask the questions necessary to remove the mystery. The answers didn't seem important. In fact, I wouldn't allow myself to even formulate the words required to create the questions themselves. Without a true question, there is no answer, nor need for any answer.

At three months Cornelia laughed. Not just a smile or a simple twist of the lips, but a genuine laugh. Sitting on the couch with my arms stretched out holding Cornelia, our eyes locked a foot away, I found myself making all sorts of noises and facial contortions. Suddenly she began to smile, and then something struck Cornelia as so damn funny she laughed out loud. It was a giggle on the inhale, short and beautiful, and it was remarkable to know that the little girl was learning something as basic as the ability to laugh. What does a tiny baby find funny, and why? She had no concept of jokes or wordplay. She couldn't fathom how ridiculous a grown man appears sitting in his shirt and tie making repetitive screeching sounds. And yet somehow Cornelia could separate sounds and faces, finding one repulsive, and the other funnier than a bag of monkeys. Every little laugh helped bury the questions in my life. They needed burying. We can fool ourselves into believing otherwise, but the primary reason we put dead people underground is to eliminate the smell.

One night the phone rang at 3 o'clock in the morning. It was early March and springtime was just around the corner. It was already warm. I had managed to negotiate my way into Ginger's bed under the theory of helping with the baby during the night. When the phone rang, I hoped it was a wrong number. Nothing good happens at 3 o'clock in the morning.

"Hello," I mumbled.

"Barry. It's Donald. I'm in some shit."

I sat up on the edge of the bed and took a moment to clear out my head.

"What kind of shit, Donald?"

"I'm in jail," he said slowly, almost like he didn't believe it yet.

"Jail? What for?"

"Well, it's not good. Can you come down here and get me out? I'm in the metro lockup."

I almost said "no."

I almost just said "no" and hung up the phone. But then I remembered my night in jail, and I felt sorry for the dumb bastard.

"O.K., I'll get dressed and get down there."

"Barry?"

"Yeah."

"Can you bring a credit card? The bail bondsman says he'll take a credit card."

There was another pause.

"All right," I said, and hung up the phone quietly. Sitting in the darkness I could hear Ginger and Cornelia breathing deep with sleep.

Donald looked even worse than he had at my office the last time I'd seen him. His head seemed small, and there were patches of facial hair like he had forgotten how to shave. After the paperwork was completed we walked together to my car. Donald slumped down in the passenger seat and buckled his seatbelt out of habit.

Before I could ask anything he said, "I've been drunk since the day I saw you. It hasn't helped much."

"What the hell happened?"

He spoke matter-of-factly, the way a person speaks when they've dulled the words through repetition. "Remember I told you that crazy woman burned my underwear? Well after I left your office I moved out of the house and got my own apartment. By the way, take a left up here."

"Where are we going?" I asked.

"To my new apartment. Anyway, I got this apartment, and bought a whole new set of underwear. A whole new set of the white kind. Take a right at the light. And that crazy woman came in my apartment. I can't prove it, but who the hell else would come into a man's house and take his underwear? Turn right again."

Donald seemed to lose his train of thought. I helped by asking, "What happened when she broke in?"

"I was in the shower. When I got out I smelled somethin' burning, went into the living room, and I could see the sliding glass door was open. Out on the balcony my gas grill was smoking. The top was closed and smoke was comin' out the sides."

Donald shook his head and said, "I opened up the top of the grill and all my underwear was on fire. Turn in the second driveway on the left. On fire. The whole pile. I couldn't save one damn pair. Not one."

I parked the car next to the pool in the space where Donald pointed. We walked upstairs together to find his apartment door wide open and the chain-lock broken. The apartment smelled like urine. Donald flicked on the lights from room to room.

He said to himself, "Probably those crazy damn brothers."

I hoped not, and was tempted to leave. Instead I said, "You can't stay here tonight. Why don't you come to my place? I'll bring you back here in the morning."

We were standing in the bedroom when I said, "It smells like piss in here."

"I wouldn't doubt it. I think I forgot to empty the jar."

"What jar?"

"The jar under the bed," Donald said.

I looked at the bed and noticed a distinct hole bored through the mattress in the center. The hole was the size of a small pancake.

"Somebody put a hole in your bed," I pointed.

"I did that," Donald answered.

"Why?"

"I've been drunk for three weeks. I got tired of gettin' outta bed to take a piss. I just sleep on my stomach and pee through the hole. I've got a jar underneath."

Donald knelt down next to the bed, reached his arm under, and pulled out a large jar three-quarters full of yellow liquid. We stood in the silent room, two men and a jar of urine.

I said, "Can we leave now?"

Donald knelt down and put the jar back in its place. I just let it happen, no words, and I pulled the door closed before we walked out together to the car.

A ways down the road Donald said, "Where you going?"

"Home. I moved in with Ginger and the baby. You can sleep on the couch. Tomorrow's Saturday. I guess I should say today's Saturday. It's already tomorrow."

I continued, "You never did tell me why you got arrested."

"When I got out of the shower I wrapped a towel around my waist. I saw my underwear on fire and just pulled off the towel and started swattin' the fire, tryin' to put it out. There was smoke everywhere, black soot. Next thing I knew the cops were there, I'm butt naked on the second floor balcony swingin' my towel around like a maniac, and all the people out by the pool are lookin' up. Little kids. Old women. One of them cops took my damn picture."

I was careful not to laugh.

Donald said mostly to himself, "It was hard to explain, you know. My underwear was on fire on the grill, and I'm naked on the balcony. They call it indecent exposure. I'm not sure what makes it indecent."

"Your ass," I blurted out, as I parked the car and turned off the headlights.

"You mean my ass, all by itself, is indecent?"

"Yes, I think so."

When we were safely inside my apartment Donald sat down on the couch. He looked lost again, unsure. Very sincerely he said, "Can I see your baby?"

It made me proud. I snuck in the bedroom and picked her up from her little bed. Cornelia's eyes opened as she adjusted to the lights in the living room. I sat down next to Donald and held the baby for him to see.

Donald said, "It's a Chinese baby," and looked at me like maybe I hadn't noticed.

It was the first time anyone I knew had used the words. The comment seemed out of place. I wondered if Cornelia would think it was funny and laugh out loud. Her squinted eyes looked at me like she was waiting for a response.

Donald asked, "Is her mother Chinese?"

"No," I answered, and then heard myself say, "my father was Oriental."

It didn't even seem like a lie. It seemed perfectly possible. Maybe my father was from Hong Kong, a successful businessman. Cornelia smiled. It was a sly, secret smile, with her head tilted slightly to the side. And then she laughed for me, and maybe for Donald, too.

Donald asked, "It doesn't bother you that you aren't sure you're the father of the baby?"

"Don't be stupid, Donald. No man is ever sure. A woman has the gift of certainty. The baby crawls out from inside her body, and she never has to wonder if her seed was involved in the miracle. Men don't get that certainty. We need a little faith. Even DNA testing is never one hundred percent."

Out of nowhere Donald said, "I wish I was you."

"What?"

"I wish I was you. Look at everything you have. You fit somewhere, right here, in this place."

It was a nice thing for him to say, but I had to consider the source. Thirty minutes earlier I watched the man replace a full jar of urine underneath his bed directly below a hole purposefully drilled in his mattress so he could pee while he slept. From Donald's current station in life, I probably looked like the King of freakin' England.

CHAPTER THIRTY

FEEDIN' GEENJA'S CAT

I received a telephone call at my office from Dr. Preston Edwards.

"Barry, this is Preston Edwards. I just wanted to touch base with you and see if you might be interested in joining us at our next meeting."

"Dr. Edwards, can I ask you a question?"

"Sure."

"Do you ever find people who figure out their own problems without the help of a support group? People who manage alone to adjust and get it all situated in their minds?"

There was a brief hesitation on the other end of the line before Dr. Edwards spoke in his calm parental tone. "Well, Barry, I have known many men, and women also, who have successfully dealt with their problems associated with genital mutilation without help. But on the other hand, I have had patients who believed they have self-healed only to have their problems resurface and manifest in acts of violence, estrangement, or sexual confusion."

I was relieved. "Doctor, I don't feel violent, estranged, or sexually confused, so maybe I'm cured."

"No one is ever really cured, Barry. We must practice preventive medicine, but also we must be prepared for the challenge of each new day."

I thought, what the hell does that mean? I said, "That's nice, Doctor, but my balls are gone, and all the sweet talk and group pity-sessions won't make 'em grow back. I'm not even sure I would want the damn things back. The only good deed they ever did was make Cornelia, and they can't honestly even take credit for that."

Dr. Edwards spoke calmly again. "Barry, I hear bitterness in your voice directed toward your testicles, and I think you hear it, too. It's the bitterness of abandonment. I've heard it before. Why don't you join us Thursday at seven o'clock? We meet at my office on Carrollton Avenue, above Larry's Fish Stick Palace, across from the school."

"Your office is above a Fish Stick Palace?" I asked.

"Yes."

"What is a Fish Stick Palace?"

"It's a restaurant, with fish sticks and french fries."

"Is it good?"

Dr. Edwards said, "I've never eaten there."

"Your office is above a Fish Stick Palace, with the aroma of fish sticks all around, and you've never eaten there? Not once?"

There was a pause. "No."

With a nasty edge I said, "I think you know where I'm going with this, Doctor. I won't be at the meeting on Thursday."

"Why not? I don't understand."

The monotone voice of Dr. Preston Edwards seemed to draw out all the smart-ass in my black heart. I remembered our first meeting at "the intervention" ending on the same sour note of rudeness.

I said, "Oh, Doctor, I think you understand perfectly well. I'll call you when I feel violent, or estranged, or sexually confused," and then I hung up the phone. The whole conversation pissed me off. The clock said 11 A.M., and I decided to leave early and go home for lunch. It was a fateful decision.

Upon entering the breezeway approaching my apartment I noticed the door wide open. Directly across the hall on the other side, Moe's door was also wide open. I stopped between the two doors. Like a flash the Chinese man flew past me from my apartment to his apartment running low and quick. I reacted in time to wedge my foot in the crack of his door before Moe could slam it shut. I threw my weight behind my shoulder up against the door and forced the opening wider, and then wider again. Moe pushed on the backside. The pressure released, and I burst inside as the little man took off across his living room. There was no furniture, and Moe ran over a suitcase, knocking him off balance enough for me to tackle the idiot.

We fell hard to the floor together, tangled up with me on top. The fool started yelling at the top of his lungs, "Hep! Hep! Hep me!"

He wriggled and kicked, wearing the same red T-shirt and bell-bottom jeans I'd seen before.

"Hep!" he yelped again. I used my size and strength to climb on top holding him down.

"What were you doin' in my apartment you son-of-a-bitch?"

"Hep me! Pweeze hep me!"

"Shut up! What were you doin' in my apartment?" I asked again.

I was sitting across his hips holding both arms tight against his chest. Moe stopped struggling and said loudly, "I feedin' Geenja's cat, Gawwie."

I growled, "You think I don't know what that means, you stupid son-of-a-bitch, 'feedin' Geenja's cat'? I'm gonna pound your fuckin' head in."

I stopped at the end of the sentence to mentally survey my situation. I was stark crazy with jealousy. Jealousy over the girl I used to call "the toad." I could feel the veins in my forehead sticking outward and the heat on my skin. The words of Dr. Preston Edwards rang in my head, "violence, estrangement, and sexual confusion." I wondered if the symptoms were progressive from left to right? Would my next emotion be the unruly desire to French-kiss the trapped Chinaman? God help us all.

We were still for a moment. There was the sound of a dog scratching on the back bedroom door. I took a moment to look around the room. The walls were bare. The only object in the entire room was the old tan suitcase behind us. I turned slightly and noticed the apartment door open to the breezeway.

Moe broke the silence, "I find peekcha of you in pawking lot."

"What?"

Moe nodded his chin toward his top T-shirt pocket. I released my grip slightly and removed a photograph from the man's pocket. It was the picture of me crawling through the bathroom window with Jennifer Farley naked in the background. I looked at the picture closely.

I whispered, "You lyin' son-of-a-bitch. You took this picture yourself. This is a different copy. There's no pin hole in this picture where it was stuck on my door."

Moe reacted to the tone of my voice and the look in my eyes. He wiggled and screamed, "Hep! Hep!" And then he yelled, "Rape! Rape!"

"What?" The words were clear and loud. I heard a noise behind me and felt the grip of strong hands on my shoulders yanking me backwards and off the screaming Asian. Lying on my back I looked up at Tom Farley and Ginger standing above. Moe scurried like a rat against the far wall and said, "He twy to wape me."

Big Tom Farley held his foot on my chest and said, "What the hell's goin' on here? What the hell?"

I explained, "I caught the son-of-a-bitch in our house. Ginger, he was in the apartment. I caught him."

Ginger, holding Cornelia, said, "He was probably feeding the cat, Barry. He likes animals, and I gave him the key to feed the cat during the day whenever I'm not home," and then she said with a slight smile, "And what does that have to do with you trying to rape the boy, anyway?"

"I wasn't trying to rape him. He's an ugly little crab. He's lying. He's a liar. Sneakin' around here all the time."

I was still lying on my back on the floor. Tom Farley, standing above, moved his eyes to my left hand resting on the floor. With a slight squeeze of the fingers I was reminded of the photograph still in the palm of my hand.

"What the hell is that?" Big Tom Farley demanded.

God was kind enough to provide to me a capsule of time, within the context of regular time, to evaluate my predicament. It was only a few seconds, but in those few seconds I was able to balance the choices. If I handed the photograph to Mr. Farley and Ginger, there would be no explanation. The consequences would surpass every idiotic or thoughtless decision I'd made since the day I heard of the Farley family. The image of the photograph would be burned in the memory of a father, and the memory of a sister, for every minute of every day of the rest of their lives, and God only knew the explanation they would receive from Jennifer.

So I ate it.

With cat-like quickness my left hand swept through the air and shoved the photograph into my wide waiting mouth. I chewed and chewed and chewed as they watched. The Chinaman stared at me like I was a circus geek gnawing the head off a rooster. There was no stopping me. I swallowed hard and the ball of sharp edges and stiff corners hung in my throat. Ginger stepped into Moe's kitchen, grabbed a glass from the first cabinet she opened, and brought me some water. We all remained silent as I sat up and finished my meal, washing it downward to the bowels below for final and complete elimination. I privately rooted for my bowels to churn and burn, the way bowels should, dreading the final passage.

From my place on the floor I looked up at Tom Farley. There was a peculiar look on his face, like he was shocked to again find himself shocked by something I had done.

Mr. Farley said, "What is the matter with you?"

I watched the big man turn and walk out the door, stopping to pick up groceries left in the breezeway. Ginger followed him out leaving me alone once again in the room with Moe. The man was squatted down against the wall with his hands on the sides of his face. We were about ten feet apart. His eyes were transfixed two feet to my right like there was a ghost sitting next to me.

"Moe, if you ever tell anyone about that photograph,

I'll kill you."

We sat that way for a while, neither of us speaking, waiting for some outward sign that the whole strange episode was over.

CHAPTER THIRTY-ONE

THE BOND OF THE IMPISH

Thursday rolled around and I found myself at seven o'clock driving to the office of Dr. Preston Edwards for his regular weekly meeting with the freaks. My outburst with Moe scared me enough to concede the possible need for outside assistance. However, I still had reservations.

The entrance to the office was on the side of the building with stairs leading to a door on the second floor with a sign painted neatly: "Dr. Preston Edwards, Psychiatric Services." The front of Larry's Fish Stick Palace below faced Carrollton Avenue, and the restaurant bustled with business.

I was met at the door by Dr. Preston Edwards himself, who seemed both surprised and overjoyed at my appearance. For a moment I had the feeling he was a mad scientist who couldn't wait to experiment with his newfound toy. I fought the visual image of being strapped to a hospital gurney in the middle of the room with electrodes attached to the shaft of my penis and the six active members of the A.A.G.A. dancing insanely around my bed.

Dr. Edwards led me to a small table in the corner of the lobby area with refreshments.

"I'm so glad you changed your mind, Barry. Sometimes the hardest part of healing is healing itself."

I wanted very badly to ask what in hell he meant. Instead, I held my tongue to the roof of my mouth and selected a sugar cookie I hoped would be chewy. I don't really like the crunchy kind.

Dr. Edwards led me to the meeting room, which was situated toward the front of the building with the semicircle of chairs next to a wall of windows overlooking the street below. I purposefully selected a seat with my back against the windows to minimize distraction. The six men were seated in exactly the same order as before.

Standing next to the chair, I asked, "Is there assigned seating?"

Dr. Edwards explained, "Actually, yes. We have found it adds external stability and provides for a more organized meeting. Coincidentally, however, the seat you selected is your assigned seat."

Kyle Pennington smiled like he had just experienced the pleasure of witnessing the power of a supernatural force leading me mystically to the proper chair. I already felt like slapping his smug little bird face. His nose was like a beak.

I scanned the room for a comrade and found Lester Bidwell in the same suit he had worn at "the intervention." Maury Knox, the guy who spoke before with his back to the group, diverted his round eyes away from mine. I remembered he had no genitals at all and caught myself looking curiously at his crotch for the sign of a bulge, any bulge at all. There was none. His navy blue corduroys were snug in the crevices.

We were all seated when Dr. Edwards spoke. "Well, gentlemen, when we met at Barry's apartment we each had the opportunity for introductions, except for you, Barry. Why don't you stand and tell us a little about yourself. A good introduction usually helps take away the jitters."

I rose slowly. All eyes were upon me, except the eyes of Maury Knox staring at my shoes.

"My name is Barry Munday. I'm thirty-three years old. I had a little accident at the theater, and the doctor removed my testicles. I don't miss 'em much, but apparently my girlfriend and my mother thought it might be a good idea to join your group. So I'm here."

I sat down. The big country boy, Bart Winfield, nodded his head up and down in a ritual of acceptance. They all followed with nods and smiles. I even got a friendly wink from Jerry Sherman, the man I remembered who had to sit down to piss like a girl. I wondered if he missed the God-given exhilaration of pulling it out and peeing in the woods the way men were blessed to do.

Dr. Edwards, seated next to me on the right, patted my back with his gentle hand as the ultimate symbol of unity. We were seven men against the world united by the strongest bond known to mankind, the bond of the outcast, the downtrodden, the impish.

And then Kyle Pennington began to speak. "Dr. Edwards, I would like to start first this evening. I had an incident at the grocery store I need to address." Birdface Pennington did not wait for permission. "I was in the coffee aisle selecting a blend. There was a man next to me, a very large man, obviously heterosexual."

I took a bite of my cookie and was disappointed at the crunch. Kyle Pennington stopped midstory and gave me a look.

"Sorry," I said.

He stared back. "I could feel the man glaring at the side of my face. The store was nearly empty, and he just stood there, a few feet away, and stared at me as I looked through the various coffees."

The story ended abruptly. I waited for more. Certainly there was more.

Dr. Edwards asked, "Kyle, why do you think he was watching you so closely?"

"I don't know. I honestly don't know."

I leaned forward in my chair, sugar cookie still firmly in hand, and said, "Excuse me. What the hell does that story have to do with our genitals? I don't get it."

Lester Bidwell laughed.

I added, "No, really. I don't get it. Did I miss something? I thought we were here to wallow in the brotherhood of mutilated genitalia, and he's telling a story about a large heterosexual man in the grocery store watching him select his coffee blend. What does that have to do with anything?"

I could feel my frustration stretch to anger.

I turned to my right to face Dr. Edwards as he spoke calmly, "Barry, we must be tolerant of what others may choose to address at our meetings. We are all very different, and obviously Kyle felt strongly about what happened to him in the grocery store."

Impulsively I answered, "You know, I wonder sometimes if everyone here actually has a problem with their private parts. I wonder if maybe we should all have a little show-and-tell. Drop our pants and prove if we really belong in this group. Put up or shut up. What do you say?"

I can't explain it now. Maybe it was a feeling, or maybe something in the corner of my eye caught my attention, but for whatever reason I turned my head to look out the front windows above Carrollton Avenue.

There she was, Lida Griggs, standing in the street below with the giant dog by her side, and next to them, unbelievably, stood Mighty Marvin, the wrestling midget. All of them were looking up at me. I stayed perfectly still as Dr. Edwards continued to speak his monotone explanation of foolishness. I haven't the slightest idea what he said. My eyes were fixed in terror on the tall woman down below, the hound from hell, and the brutal midget who owed me money. The beast began to bark.

My mind flew. Had they hunted me down, followed me to the meeting, three cars behind, darting through traffic? Or was this happenstance? Had they simply stepped out for a delicious dinner of fish sticks and french fries and found themselves recognizing the back of my head in the window above the restaurant? I felt the sugar cookie fall from my hand.

Dr. Edwards said, "Barry, is everything O.K.?"

"No," I whispered, "everything's not O.K."

I could hear the sounds around me of people standing from their chairs and moving toward the window to see what I could see outside.

From the look on Lida's face I could tell her bitterness and scorn had not subsided since the day in the restaurant when she punched me in the stomach. In fact, as her face tightened, locked in the stare, I could see her hatred of me had reached biblical proportions, and God knows how she teamed up with Mighty Marvin. With all the men in the group peering through the window, Lida raised her arm slowly, cocked her hand, and flipped me the bird.

"Who is that?" Maury Knox uttered behind me.

I stood. Lida and the dog immediately reacted and galloped around the side of the building toward the stairs, Marvin trailing behind. I ran through the meeting room and into the lobby to the front door. I swung open the door wildly to see the possessed woman and her traveling circus coming up the stairs. I slammed the door closed, turned the deadbolt, and looked up to see all the members of the A.A.G.A. standing together at the entrance of the meeting room.

Dr. Edwards asked, "Barry, is everything all right?"

There was a pounding on the door beside me.

In a panic I asked, "Do the front windows open? Do they open?"

Dr. Edwards replied, "Yes, they do open. But maybe we should stop and discuss this situation, Barry. Running away never solves anything."

As sarcastic as possible I said, "I believe you gentlemen already have your hands full with Kyle's problem in the grocery store. It might take all night to figure that one out."

My tone changed to angry. "Now listen, you crazy bastards, I'm goin' out the front window. When you see me go, open the door and let these people in. Try to keep them busy for thirty seconds. That's all I'm askin'. Can you do it?"

Lester Bidwell said, "Hell, yeah. Go boy, go."

I ran back to the front windows near the chairs, stepping squarely on the crunchy cookie on the floor. I could still hear Lida and Marvin beating frantically on the door and the giant dog barking his brains out. I crawled through the second-story window, gave Lester Bidwell the thumbs up, and slid down a drain pipe beside the awning of Larry's Fish Stick Palace. I peeked around the corner. There was no sign of trouble on the stairs. Lester Bidwell had done his job, and done it well. I ran like a free man to my car and sped away in the night.

CHAPTER THIRTY-TWO

CIRCLES

The beginning of April finally arrived and Cornelia was four months old. She seemed to know her name, searching for the face of the person saying "Cornelia," eyes drifting and stopping on the eyes of the person speaking to her, and then laughing like the room was full of clowns. It made me wonder what kind of baby I had been. Fat or skinny. Happy or dull. It seemed obvious to me that Cornelia was far ahead of other babies, destined to walk and talk months before her peers, though I had nothing to compare her to. She was incomparable.

"Mom, I never hear you talk about me as a baby. I've never seen any of my baby pictures."

"I don't remember much," my mother said. "It goes so fast. One day I was holding you in my arms, and the next day it seemed you were off to school, and then all grown up."

She went to her bedroom and came out with a shoe box. We sat at the kitchen table, Cornelia's back held against my chest, her head under my chin. My mother reached her hand inside the box and pulled out photographs.

I was a fat baby. Fat little legs and big cheeks. My mother smiled with delight as she pulled out another picture of me under the Christmas tree, dressed like an elf, with wrapping paper and bows everywhere. She held the picture up next to the face of Cornelia.

"She's got your eyes, and your mouth."

I looked at the picture closely, and then at the baby's face, but I couldn't see it. Maybe men can't see such things. Maybe men aren't supposed to identify their children by sight. I smelled her head, clean and fresh, with little wisps of dark hair.

My mother said, "And she's got your toes, too."

I pulled off my shoe and sock, taking a long look at my big ugly toes, a patch of hair on the biggest, and the remnants of an ingrown toenail. The little toe was crooked and wedged up snug against the fourth toe. No one pays attention to that fourth toe. I looked at Cornelia's perfect little feet, and then back at my own. They didn't seem to be from the same species, much less the same family.

My mother kept pulling out pictures and little trinkets.

"You were a good baby, Barry. Always smilin'. I couldn't figure out what was so funny, but you were always smilin' about somethin' or other."

She held up a picture for me to see. I was maybe two or three years old, sitting on the floor by a refrigerator, covered with purple jelly.

Mother said, "I went outside to get the mail. I remember the lady next door stopped to talk, just for a few minutes. When I got back inside you had grape jelly everywhere. You said you were makin' us lunch. Jelly sandwiches."

My mother looked like she might cry. She said, "I sat down on the floor next to you and we ate grape jelly sandwiches together. Just me and you."

Cornelia giggled at nothing. A thin line of clear drool spanned the short distance from her mouth to the kitchen table.

"It never bothered you that we were poor. It never bothered you that we were alone. I was always worried for you, growin' up without a father, but I don't think you missed him until you were older, until you needed to ask questions about being a man and there was no one to ask."

My mother peered into the box and shuffled her old hands through the remaining photographs.

"The world goes in circles, you know. That's the way it is. I don't just mean it goes in circles around the sun, or from day to night. I mean our lives go in circles, all our lives. Crazy people don't see the circles. They think in straight lines. If you can't see the circles, you can't find yourself."

I finally said, "I wish I could remember sitting on the floor in the kitchen eating jelly sandwiches with you."

My mother smiled. "There's a lot more to memory than being able to see a picture in your head. Believe me, you remember everything you do and everything you hear from the day you're born until the day you die. It's all in there somewhere."

My mother pulled another photograph from the box. It was a picture of me in my grandmother's lap. I called her Honey. She died when I was five.

"When your grandmother was in the hospital, waiting to die those last few weeks, she was amazed at the memories that came back. She made me sit by the bed for hours on end while she went through her head like a file cabinet and told me things she had long since forgotten. Parts of conversations from forty years before, lines from movies, everything she got for Christmas when she was ten years old. In those few weeks I just sat and watched her live her life again in her mind, laughing and crying like it was all brand new, crystal clear."

My mother smiled to herself and shook her head. "But you know what? Her mind was perfect except for one thing. She believed her father was still alive. He'd been dead for twenty-five years, but she would stop in the middle of a sentence and say, 'Daddy's coming to take me to dinner. We're going to that place across town.' I'd say, 'Momma, Poppa's been dead twenty-five years,' and she'd say, 'Oh, don't be silly, he'll be here any minute,' and she'd fix her hair."

I asked, "Did Honey ever come to her senses?"

"Oh, she already had her senses. She just decided her daddy wasn't dead, and that was that. I'd say, 'Momma, what year is this? And what year was I born? And so what year did Poppa die?' But you can't trick a person like that. She turned back the clock, made a few changes, and brought her daddy to her deathbed."

Cornelia began to fidget. She sucked on her hand and kicked her little legs. I put my face up against the side of her face and rejoiced in the idea she might remember this day, her grandmother telling stories, my face warm against her cheek. We were quiet, and then Cornelia laughed again.

"Ginger's a good mother, Barry. I've watched her take care of the baby."

We were quiet again for a long spell, just watching the baby, until I couldn't wait any longer. "Mom, are there any pictures of my father in that box?"

Not taking her eyes from the child, my mother said, "No, I don't have any pictures of your father."

"I need to know something, Mom. I need to know if he knew I was born, if he knew you were pregnant, when he left. That's all I need to know."

My mother thought a moment and answered. "That's just the first question, Barry. Either answer sends you in a direction, doesn't it? If I tell you your daddy knew I was pregnant, knew you were born, and walked away from us, you'll make yourself crazy wondering why, wondering what was wrong with us, or wrong with him.

"If I tell you he never knew I was pregnant, never knew you came into this world, you'll make yourself crazy wondering where he is, who he is.

"You have to find the place in your mind where it doesn't matter. Leaving your sperm behind doesn't make a man a father any more than the first brick makes a house. You've built your own house now. Before you had Cornelia, did you know there was love like that in this whole world?"

I turned the baby around to face me. Her eyes started at my chest and traveled slowly upward to my own eyes. We stayed that way, just looking at each other, and I wondered who she would be, and who I would be through her. Many years later, on her own private death bed, would she conjure me up among the living, to be there with her when she needed me the most? Yes, she would.

CHAPTER THIRTY-THREE

A GOOD SURPRISE

After the conversation with my mother I spent a few days thinking about the things she said. I was sitting in my office minding my own business when Lonnie Green made one of his daily appearances at my door.

"Good mornin', Top Dog," he chirped.

"Good mornin', Lonnie."

"Got a minute?"

"Come in."

He sat down across from my desk and studied me for a moment. Finally he said, "You've been doin' a helluva job lately. It's time you got a raise."

"O.K."

"And a better office," he added. "This office is depressing. Let's move you in the conference room down the hall. It's got a big window and space to spread out."

I felt a twitch of pride. It was a strange feeling. For some reason my instincts told me to remain indifferent, aloof from the rewards of Lonnie Green and the insurance business, but I'd been working long hours, and we both knew I'd earned this reward.

As he was leaving my office, Lonnie turned and said, "Oh, by the way, I need you to stay late this evening. Martin Lefleur is supposed to call around six or six-thirty, and I need you here to take the call and walk him through the proposal. Me and the wife got a party to go to, and I can't be here."

I agreed to stay late and wait for the call. Through the

day I moved everything in my office down the hall. Over the past several months I had accumulated pictures of Cornelia and Ginger, a wall plaque from a fancy seminar in Baton Rouge, and other odds and ends. In just a few hours sitting in my new office I could barely remember how dark and small the old office had been. It was now a dark and small conference room. For whatever reason, Lucy, the receptionist, didn't seem pleased with my promotion. She said I was getting too big for my britches. Maybe she was beginning to regret her decision to reject my early advances. Maybe not. Still, there were times I stole a peek at her skirt when her head was turned. No harm done.

Six o'clock rolled around and the office was empty. Ginger had called to let me know dinner would be ready when I got home around seven. I finished my paperwork and waited for Martin Lefleur to call. I waited past 6:30 and tried to remember when Lonnie had said the man was supposed to call. I waited until 6:45, and finally the phone broke the silence.

"Hello."

"Barry?"

"Yes."

"This is Lonnie. Martin caught me on my cell phone. You can get outta there. Go home, see you tomorrow."

And he hung up.

I drove home hoping Ginger had made her famous tacos. My mouth watered at the thought of the first bite of the crunchy shell filled with spicy meat, onions, cheese, and hot sauce. It was a warm evening, and I walked from the car across the parking lot with my jacket over my arm.

There was a pang of frustration when I tried the doorknob and found it locked. I rooted through my pockets for the keys, dropped them on the ground, cussed twice, and shoved the key in the door.

It was completely dark inside. No smell of tacos. I cussed again, flipped on the light, and "SURPRISE!"

The scream shook my heart and sent my back against the wall.

The living room was full of people. All the faces I knew. A giant banner across the wall said, "HAPPY BIRTHDAY BARRY."

I had completely forgotten my birthday, April 7th, thirty-four years old. There was a gigantic cake on the kitchen table, wrapped presents, birthday decorations, and everyone had birthday hats and whistles.

I was speechless. I saw the faces of Ginger, the Farleys, Newton Creech, Jennifer, Lonnie Green and his wife ,Patty, my mother, Lucy, Dr. Shriver, the guy named Joey from the rehearsal dinner, Moe, Dr. Preston Edwards and his sidekicks, Father Walsh, and Cornelia. They were everywhere at once. It was crazy shit.

My eyes were wide and my back was still against the wall next to the open door when Ginger brought me the baby and the room erupted into the "Happy Birthday" song. The noise and whistles scared the baby and she cried until the final line. I must say, it was the first and only surprise party in my life, and it surprised the holy shit out of me. If I had been a few years older I might have fallen over dead of a heart attack before the song was over. With their enthusiasm, I think they would have waited until they were finished to administered CPR. Lying dead on the floor, I would have missed the tail end of the song.

Ginger gave me a big kiss on the lips in front of everyone. Donald stepped up with a woman to greet me.

"Happy birthday, man. This is my wife, Sandy."

"Your wife?"

"Yeah, we got back together. They call it reconciliation. Her crazy brothers, Toby and Elvis, should be here in a few minutes."

Sandy extended her hand, and I shook it lightly. Donald had his arm around her like a schoolboy. I tried to picture Sandy's face as it must have looked when she lit Donald's underwear ablaze. And now they were back together as if nothing had ever happened.

Music began to play and conversations rose around the room. It was hard to believe all these people were in the same place at the same time. I handed the baby back to Ginger. Lonnie Green approached with his wife.

"You fell for the late phone call trick, didn't you? Martin Lefleur. That son-of-a-bitch never calls. You should've known that. Happy birthday, Bubba."

Lonnie's wife gave me a hug and held on a second too long. I felt her tremendous breasts pressed against my chest. Lonnie either didn't notice or didn't care.

I made a move toward the bathroom and found myself by the kitchen table next to Joey and Newton Creech. My timing was a bit too perfect.

Joey said, "Hey, I've got something for you."

From his pocket he pulled out Newton's eyepatch, folded like it had been in his pocket since the day I gave it to him.

As Newton reached for the patch, I quickly announced,

"I've got to go to the bathroom."

Newton took the patch and gently unfolded the corners like it was painful. As I headed away I heard Joey say, "Sorry, man. I accidentally washed it in the washing machine. But I wore it one day, just to freak people out."

The next group I passed was Dr. Preston Edwards and the members of the A.A.G.A. They were huddled in a corner with Tom Farley. I made no eye contact and slithered past, hearing big Tom Farley ask, "So how do you boys know Barry?" The potential for disaster was unlimited.

I spent longer in the bathroom than necessary, gathering myself and laughing out loud at the thought of my surprise birthday party. I heard a noise on the other side of the locked door and saw a photograph slide under the bottom of the door across the tile floor. It was another copy of the picture of me in the bathroom window with Jennifer stark naked in the background. I took a private moment to examine her nakedness closely and saw the pin hole on the top of the picture where it had been stuck to my door. God bless double prints. I hoped it was the last copy as I tore it up and flushed it away. I was left to wonder who had pushed it under the door, when I heard a soft knock. I unlocked the door and eased it open. I was knocked backwards by the force of someone entering upon me. Mighty Marvin thrust his hard, compact body inside and slammed the door behind him. We were only a few feet apart. I felt my anger for the little man rise, and then he said, "I owe you some money."

He pulled a wad of green cash from his back pocket and removed the red rubber band that held the wad tight.

His fat little nubs fingered the money, removing several bills.

"Sorry about the misunderstanding," he said, and held the money out to me. I reached to take the cash I deserved. At the exact moment the bathroom door pushed open again, forcing Mighty Marvin up against me, his head belt-level. Tom Farley stepped through the door to see me, the father of his grandchild, up against a midget, exchanging cash in the bathroom with the door closed. We all just stood there for a moment in that small room.

Mighty Marvin, still smelling like meat products, waddled past the legs of big Tom Farley and out the door. We were alone. I started to say, "He owed me some money. We got in a fight at a gay bar, and he stuck me with the bill." I actually put the words together in my head, a fine explanation, but instead of saying anything out loud I just walked past Mr. Farley carefully and closed the door behind me as I left.

Near the refrigerator I encountered Father Walsh and Moe. They were involved in a conversation, believe it or not, and stopped as I reached for a beer. Moe's eyes grew large.

Father Walsh extended his hand. "Happy birthday, young man."

"Thank you."

We shook hands, and then Moe, perhaps feeling safe with a priest nearby, stuck out his bony little hand for a shake. There was a moment of hesitation, not unnoticed by Father Walsh, before I took the girlish hand and shook. I squeezed tightly, sending a signal of physical dominance, but careful not to overemphasize the point. Moe smiled, and I couldn't help but smile back as his eyes focused directly at Father Walsh, two feet to my right.

Dr. Edwards called me aside near the front door with Maury Knox. They seemed excited and nervous. Dr. Edwards said, "Barry, we have a surprise guest tonight. They should be here any minute."

Before the words could leave his mouth, there was a knock on the door. I figured it was Toby and Elvis. I hoped they weren't still mad about the night at the Beaver Tree. I opened the door and screamed. It was a high-pitched Halloween scream escaping from my throat before I could think about it.

Lida Griggs stood at the door. She was dressed in black with her hair neatly in a bun. I peeked around the corner but the dog was nowhere in sight. Lida stood perfectly still, hands crossed at her waist, and the only sound behind me was the low hum of Simon & Garfunkel. My scream had stopped each conversation, and I imagined all heads had turned my direction.

Dr. Preston Edwards came up beside me, put his loving arm around my shoulder, and spoke calmly, "Barry, after you left the other night, the group embraced Lida. It was the best session we've had in years. Four hours long. She's reached a peace in her life. She's happy for you, Barry, and wanted to be here for your birthday party. I feel it's an important part of the healing process for both of you. Besides, Lida and Kyle Pennington have started a relationship."

I laughed. Not out of spite, just imagining Kyle Pennington running from that gigantic dog across the white sands of a beach in his bathing suit, looking over his shoulder. Or Mighty Marvin holding Kyle in a death-grip headlock on the steps of the hotel pool.

Without a word I turned back to the party. In the middle of the room Ginger asked me, "Who is that?"

I answered, "Kyle Pennington's girlfriend."

Kyle was standing nearby. I turned and said to him, "Congratulations."

With humble sincerity Kyle Pennington said, "Thank you."

I laughed again, and couldn't stop smiling for the rest of the night. Toby and Elvis arrived. They followed Jennifer around like puppies. Toby eventually asked me, "Hey, Barry, is that the rabbit-girl from the strip joint? That's gotta be her. I swear to God."

We looked at Jennifer together. "I don't think so, Toby."

Lida and Kyle Pennington held hands. Joey got very drunk and asked Newton Creech to give the eyepatch back. He wouldn't do it. Moe, with his red T-shirt and bell-bottom jeans, kept his distance and eventually disappeared. Toby and Elvis paid Lester Bidwell fifty bucks to see his deformed genitalia with one testicle above his penis, and one below. They paid another fifty bucks to take a picture. Jerry Sherman took offense and found himself later in the night tied to a tree next to the railroad tracks behind the apartment complex.

I ended up late in the evening standing in the kitchen with Jennifer. A few people had gone home. I was slightly drunk.

"Jennifer, when I first met Ginger, I thought she was crazy. But she's nothing compared to the rest of you people."

We both looked around the room at the leftover oddballs.

Jennifer turned to me, as pretty as ever, and out of character said, "Sometimes we get so comfortable with our own craziness we begin to believe we're normal, we're the standard of normalcy. We dig our own ruts and then lose perspective."

"What do you mean?" I asked. I just wanted to stand next to her a few more minutes.

"Well, was your life normal before Cornelia? Dedicating yourself to the physical sex act, like a dog in the yard? Going to strip joints, ignoring your family, ignoring your friendships, your job? Of course not, Barry. Look around the room. You're one of the strangest people here, easily."

I looked around the room again at the faces of Dumb Donald and his underwear-burning wife, Maury Knox (the man with no genitals), and Lida Griggs. I wondered, when they look at me, who do they see?

"Jennifer, was that you on the stage that night at the Beaver Tree?"

I thought maybe I had stumbled upon a moment of weakness.

She answered, "Barry, if you're gonna call another person's bluff, maybe you should pay more attention to your watch."

Excitedly I said, "I knew it. I knew it. It was eleven o'clock, not ten o'clock. Am I right?"

There was no answer. We stood next to each other for a few moments saying nothing. I knew she had given me all I would get.

Finally I said, "Well, you might think I'm strange, but at least I know I'm not as weird as you."

Jennifer smiled and whispered to me, "Barry, that's what a family is. A bunch of weird people who care about each other."

After everyone left I fell asleep in Ginger's arms with Cornelia's tiny hand wrapped around my finger.

CHAPTER THIRTY-FOUR

ONE MAN'S BURDEN

Life is a strange place. There are lots of ways to get there from here. My story didn't really begin until I was thirty-three years old. Some people's stories never begin.

I impregnated one of the last random women I conquered before my testicles vanished from the face of this Earth. I never stopped to consider whether she would be a good mother for my child, or even whether I would be able to sit in the same room with the woman after the sex act was completed. And yet, somehow, through this disconnected senselessness, without even the faintest memory of the act itself, I set in motion a chain reaction of happiness.

Ginger and I got married and adopted two more children. I was allowed (sort of) to name the third one, Haywood, and he carries my last name. I became partners with Lonnie Green, and he says next year he'll retire and the business will be mine. I'll believe it when it happens.

Ginger and Cornelia saved my life. Not from a burning building, or suicide, but from a life of never knowing. Given the choice, I would never have had a child. I sometimes think about the day I was buried in my cave at the St. Charles Guest House, rolled up on the couch, alone, feeling sorry for myself, letting my hand drift down between my legs to make sure I wasn't dreaming. I remember getting the letter from Newton Creech and reading every word. Before I could think about it, before I could poison the reaction, I was overjoyed.

Overjoyed at the idea of a new life, part of me, somewhere in this world, waiting on the verge of possibility. I guess one man's burden is another man's pleasure. At least that's what Dr. Edwards and the boys say on Thursday nights at seven o'clock above Larry's Fish Stick Palace on Carrollton Avenue.

ACKNOWLEDGMENTS

The greatest gift a writer can be given is the gift of freedom. It's not money, or a fancy award, or a good review. It's freedom. The freedom to write whatever the hell I want to write, and then see it on a bookshelf or in the hands of a stranger at the airport. I am given this freedom by my wonderful family, the folks at my law firm, and MacAdam/Cage Publishing Company. I would be a fool not to acknowledge and appreciate this gift.

Goofy people who contributed to this book include Bluto Shannon, Crunchy Howard, Big Top Strecker, Jimbo Gilbert, The Book Troll, David "Fine Ass" Poindexter, my friend Pat Walsh, Ludlow Dasinger, John David Whetstone, Big Daddy, Wild Bill Conway, Shroeder Gibbons, Hal Parisienne, Bill Borchert, Eddie Cummings, Brian Dasinger, Crazy Kyle Jennings and Jill, Dad and Virginia, Mom and Skip, Rodney, Paige, Melissa and James, Sharon, The Alabama Booksmith, Martin, Todd Coverdale, Mark Dunn, Melanie, Amy, Tasha, Dorothy for the cool book cover, J. P., Dennis Hilton, and of course, Barry Munday.

ABOUT THE AUTHOR

Frank Turner Hollon has written four published novels: *The Pains of April, The God File, A Thin Difference,* and *Life is a Strange Place.* His novels have been selected by BookSense as well as the Barnes & Noble's Discover Great New Writers program. Two of Frank's short stories have appeared in *Stories from the Blue Moon Café, Volumes I* and *II.*

Frank lives and practices law in Baldwin County, Alabama. He spends a great deal of time avoiding questions about the strange books he has written.